Lacey pitch ... et went flying.

Only at the last second did she catch herself and somehow manage to keep from landing face-first in the dirt.

"Whoa! Nice save!"

Oh, sure, *now* he noticed her.

Lacey stood straight again, brushing her hands together and retrieving her shoe with a yank to get the heel unstuck from the dirt.

When she was finally put back together, she looked up to see that the man she assumed to be Seth Camden had her jacket and was glancing in her direction.

The Camden blue eyes—Lacey did recall mention of those somewhere.

Since they went with a face that was drop-dead gorgeous enough to steal her breath, for a moment all she could do was stare.

"Are you all right?"

"I'm fine," Lacey said, coming to her senses. "Are you Seth Camden?"

"In the flesh."

Don't get me started thinking about that!

Dear Reader,

Lacey Kincaid has something to prove to the sexist father who favored her two brothers, and she's just been given the opportunity to do that. She's come to Northbridge, Montana, to oversee the building of the training center for her father's newly acquired football team. It's a huge job, but she's determined to do it no matter how many twenty-hour days she has to work to accomplish it.

Seth Camden is a laid-back cowboy who runs a Northbridge ranch and the rest of the notorious Camden family's agricultural holdings out of a country mansion. He's turned off by Lacey's obsession with her job. Too bad he's so turned on by Lacey.

But he is, and he can't help himself. And even though the last thing Lacey needs is a distraction, that's just what she gets in the form of the oh-so-sexy Camden cowboy.

I hope you enjoy just one more visit to my small town.

Happy reading!

Victoria Pade

THE CAMDEN
COWBOY

VICTORIA PADE

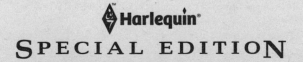

SPECIAL EDITION

Recycling programs
for this product may
not exist in your area.

ISBN-13: 978-0-373-65676-9

THE CAMDEN COWBOY

VICTORIA PADE

is a *USA TODAY* bestselling author of numerous romance novels. She has two beautiful and talented daughters—Cori and Erin—and is a native of Colorado, where she lives and writes. A devoted chocolate lover, she's in search of the perfect chocolate-chip-cookie recipe. For information about her latest and upcoming releases, and to find recipes for some of the decadent desserts her characters enjoy, log on to www.vikkipade.com.

Chapter One

Great—figures this would be a day I'm in a skirt and high heels...

Lacey Kincaid sighed as she pulled her sedan to the side of a dirt road and turned off the car's engine.

She'd been driving down one backcountry Montana road after another in search of Seth Camden for the last hour of her Wednesday afternoon. She'd found his house and was told that he was out fixing fences and how to find him. The man was not easy to get to even *with* directions.

And now that she'd made it to the part of the Camden ranch where she'd been told she could find him, he still wasn't going to be easy to get to. Particularly not when she was going to have to drop down about two feet from the roadside and cross several yards of field to actually reach him. And she was going to have to do it in a skirt and three-inch heels.

But today was the day Lacey needed to talk to him, and today—right now—was when she was going to talk to him.

This would, however, be the first time she'd met Seth Camden—or any member of the infamous Camden family. With that in mind, she wanted to be certain of her appearance, so she flipped down the visor that was just above her head and peered into it.

For work, she always wore her pale blond, shoulder-length hair swept back. She did it loosely and with a sporty look to it because she didn't want to appear stark or severe, but she was all business and she didn't want anyone thinking differently because of some unconscious hair toss that might give a different impression.

For the meeting to discuss financials that had taken up most of her second day in the small town of Northbridge, Montana, she'd twisted her hair into a knot and let some wispy ends cascade from the top. Checking it out in the visor mirror now she could tell that it was all still the way she'd done it that morning, so she didn't touch it.

She also avoided wearing too much makeup. A dusting of blush along the apples of her high cheekbones, a hint of lip gloss on her already rosy lips and a few swipes of mascara to color her lashes and accentuate her green eyes, and she was out the door in the morning. *Dolling* herself up—that's what her father would have called it if she did any more than that. And it would defeat her every purpose, because in Morgan Kincaid's view she would be just another ineffective woman more devoted to her vanity and nabbing a husband than to the job she'd been given.

Satisfied with her appearance, Lacey flipped the

visor up again and got out of her car. She was wearing business clothes—a cotton blouse underneath a tailored coat that matched her straight, gray, knee-length skirt with its slit in the back to accommodate walking.

At least it accommodated walking anywhere but across the rutted dirt road to the other side, where she awkwardly hopped down the slope from the road to the field.

Teetering, she barely retained her footing as she got down into the gully. But once she was there, she did her best to walk with some semblance of dignity and headed for the man who didn't seem to have noticed he was no longer alone.

It didn't strike her as strange that he hadn't noticed her. He was replacing a section of fence that had collapsed somehow. His back was to her and to the road where she'd parked. Plus he was so far from the road that she doubted he'd even heard her car.

Lacey's right ankle buckled just then and she veered wildly to one side. She didn't fall, but it was close, and she checked to make sure she hadn't broken the heel off of her shoe.

She hadn't, so she continued on, focused on the man who was her goal.

A grayish-white cowboy hat was her only view of him from the neck up, but below that he was dressed in a white crewneck T-shirt, jeans and cowboy boots. Lacey could tell that he was tall even from where she was— over six feet tall, she judged. And he had broad, broad shoulders that she watched expand when his massively muscled arms rose in the air, lifting a posthole digger from out of the hole he was working on.

He gripped the handles of the X-shaped tool in his

leather-work-gloved hands and he pivoted slightly to his left with it. He pressed the handles together to open the blue steel head at the opposite end, releasing the dirt he'd taken from the hole. Then he drew the handles apart, pivoted to his original stance and stabbed the closed head into the hole once more.

As she approached, he stood with his legs apart. Long legs that were thick enough to test the denim of his jeans. Even from a distance she could tell that the twin pockets of those jeans cupped a rear end that rivaled the best she'd ever seen. And being in contact with the players on her father's new football team—the Montana Monarchs—Lacey had seen some great ones.

Another near tumble almost landed her on her own rear end but she managed to keep herself upright, returning her gaze to Seth Camden as she continued on.

His back was straight and strong, and while the white T-shirt he was wearing wasn't tight, it was damp with the sweat of working in the sun on an August day and it clung to him like a second skin. It clung to back muscles that any athlete she knew would have envied. Well-honed muscles that narrowed gracefully to a taut waist. And that rear end again…

Okay, enough of that! she told herself, as she began to draw nearer. Near enough, she thought, to shout, "Excuse me…"

But either she wasn't near enough or her timing was bad because rather than respond, he again jabbed the posthole digger into the ground.

Feeling the August heat herself, Lacey paused long enough to remove her suit jacket, fold it neatly in half and place it over her arm. Thank goodness her cotton blouse was sleeveless because it was blazing hot out there.

Despite the heat and the terrain, when the daughter of football legend Morgan Kincaid set her mind to something, she followed through. So once she'd taken off her jacket, she forged ahead—this time keeping her gaze high enough to take in the man's substantial neck peeking from beneath the brim of the cowboy hat.

A Camden who was a cowboy—that seemed like a contradiction when the Camden family was renowned in the business world.

Lacey's own father had parlayed his professional football fame and fortune into an impressive empire that encompassed retail, rental and hotel properties, car dealerships and various other businesses along with his newest venture—owning an NFL expansion franchise.

But Camden Incorporated? If Camden was like a giant, lush bowl of fruit, the Kincaid Corporation would equal one small stem of grapes on a single cluster in the Camden bowl.

The stores that bore the Camden name were the superstores of all superstores. With multiple locations in every state and in several other countries, they had no equals. The Camden stores put under one roof almost every item and service the consumer wanted or needed at the lowest prices that could be had. They advertised that an entire house could be built, finished, furnished, landscaped and lived in for a lifetime without the owner ever needing to step foot in another store. Even banking, legal and health needs could be seen to there.

But behind the stores themselves, the Camdens owned much of what supplied the products they sold—factories, manufacturers, farms, ranches, dairies, timberland, lumber mills, bottling plants, and numerous other production-level businesses and industries that facilitated their low prices. They also had a hand in distribution centers and had now added a network of medical, dental and vision clinics to each store to go along with pharmacies that offered low-cost prescriptions—because they even owned pharmaceutical companies and research facilities.

There just wasn't much the Camdens *didn't* have a hand in, so it was surprising to find one of the ten grandchildren who now ran Camden Incorporated acting like a small-town cowboy.

Not that she knew the intricacies of the family, because she didn't. An entire section of a course she'd taken in college had been devoted to studying the business model of Camden Incorporated, but when it came to the Camdens themselves, only H. J. Camden—Seth Camden's great-grandfather and the founder of the business—and H.J.'s son, Hank, who would have been Seth Camden's grandfather, had been discussed.

The present-day Camdens tended to crop up occasionally in the news in conjunction with charities they sponsored. But beyond that they kept a very low profile, and Lacey couldn't name them or what any of them did.

Still, it seemed strange that a member of a family like that would be out here working in the hot sun digging postholes.

"Excuse me…" she tried again.

But no sooner had the words come out of her mouth than she raised one foot to take another step and lost her shoe completely, costing her precious balance.

In fact this time she pitched forward, her jacket went flying and only at the last second did she catch herself and somehow manage to keep from landing face-first in the dirt.

"Whoa! Nice save!"

Oh, sure, *now* he noticed her.

Lacey stood straight again, brushing her hands together to get the dirt off of them and retrieving her shoe with a yank to get the heel unstuck. Then she brushed the dirt off her bare foot, replaced her shoe and rubbed her hands together again.

When she was finally put back together she looked up to find that Seth Camden—if that was who he was—had abandoned his hole digger and gloves, and was picking up her jacket. It had flown off her arm and landed on the ground a few feet away.

He grabbed her jacket, shook the soil from it and then stood up to look in her direction.

The Camden blue eyes—Lacey did recall mention of those somewhere. Now she knew why they were noteworthy; when her gaze met his, the sight of bright, brilliant cobalt eyes staring quizzically back at her was something to see.

And since they went with a face that was drop-dead gorgeous enough to steal her breath, for a moment all Lacey could do was stare.

With his sharply drawn, chiseled features, the man before her couldn't have been more handsome if he'd tried. He had a squarish jaw and chin, a perfectly shaped mouth with lips that were full but not too full, a just-long-enough nose. And those eyes peering at her from beneath a straight, strong brow.

"Are you all right?" he asked in a deep voice that was so masculine it made very girly goose bumps erupt along the surface of her skin, even in the summer heat.

"Oh. Fine. I'm fine," Lacey said, coming to her senses. "Are you Seth Camden?"

"In the flesh."

Don't get me started thinking about that!

"Did you come all the way out here looking for me?" he asked, that brow furrowing from beneath his hat.

He took his hat off and ran the back of his hand across his forehead. There was an inexplicable sexiness to that gesture. His hair was the dark, rich color of espresso coffee beans, and was cropped short and close to his head on the sides, with the top left just long enough to be swept back in a careless mass of waves and spikes. And he didn't have hat-hair.

Then the Stetson went on again, and the blue eyes were once more leveled at her.

Just then she realized that he'd asked her a question and was probably waiting for an answer. She'd been so lost in gawking at him.

"I went to your house first. I found someone at one of your barns to tell me where you were and how to get to you. I needed to speak with you, so—"

"Here you are," he finished for her. "What can I do for you…? Or maybe you can tell me who you are first…?"

Another bit of negligence. Lacey wasn't ordinarily so flustered, and she didn't understand why she was now. She just hoped it would stop.

"I'm sorry. I'm Lacey Kincaid—"

"I've met Morgan Kincaid—he and I did the closing on the property he just bought from us. And Ian and Hutch Kincaid—they've been around town—"

"Morgan is my father. Ian and Hutch are my older brothers. I don't know if my father told you or not, but the property he bought from you is to be used as the new training center for the Monarchs—"

"Right, your father's football team."

"And the project has been given to me to manage." Lacey hadn't intended to sound so proud of that fact, but it was such a big deal to her she couldn't ever seem to say it without sounding pleased with herself.

"And that's what you want to talk to *me* about?" he asked, handing her her jacket as he did.

Lacey accepted it and went on. "There are three things I wanted to talk to you about," she said in her best I'm-the-boss-and-this-is-all-business tone. "I just got into town yesterday and I'm staying in an apartment Hutch owns. But it's in Northbridge and it takes me fifteen minutes to get from there to the site—"

"Fifteen minutes is an eternity to you?"

That *was* the way she'd said it. "It would just be better if I could be closer, and I've been told that the nearest thing to the site is your place, and that you have a guesthouse. I was wondering if you might be interested in renting it?"

"To you? For you to live in?"

"It would just be me, yes. And I would hardly be there except to sleep because this project is going to keep me on-site the rest of the time. You probably wouldn't even know I was there."

"Oh, I think I would…"

Lacey had no idea what that meant but it had come with a hint of a smile that curled only the left side of his mouth. A smile that was even sexier than the brow wipe had been.

But why things like that were even occurring to her,

she had no idea. She opted to ignore the phenomena and go on as if she hadn't heard his comment.

"I only need somewhere to sleep and shower and change clothes, really. And of course I'll pay rent—"

"You'd need a kitchen, too, wouldn't you? How else would you fix meals without a kitchen?" he asked, giving no indication whether or not the guesthouse *did* have a kitchen, merely seeming curious. In a laid-back, slightly amused way that was also sexy but still a little frustrating to Lacey.

"Okay, yes, a kitchen—or just a kitchenette where I could make coffee would be nice—but most days I eat whatever I can order in at the site," she answered, as if it were inconsequential. "And if you had some pressing need for your guesthouse while I'm using it, I could always spend a night or two with one of my brothers. If it was absolutely necessary—"

"And make that *looong* fifteen-minute commute?"

He was clearly teasing her because he'd said that with a full smile. A very engaging smile.

But Lacey was sweltering in that sun and didn't have time to waste admiring his smile, so she said, "Yes," as if his question had been serious. "The second thing I needed to talk to you about is the house and barn on the property we bought from you—"

"Yeah, we thought long and hard about getting rid of those. My great-grandfather was born in that house, his father used the barn as a lumber mill and that was where my great-grandfather started the business. As kids when we'd visit here we'd have sleepovers in the old place. But since nobody's used anything over there since we were all kids, and since the land is played out both for crops and for grazing, we decided to sell."

"Yes, well," Lacey said, impatient with the family history. "There are some things still in the attic in the house and in the barn—"

"There are? I thought we got everything out."

"Apparently not. Since they're your family's belongings, you should be the one to go through them, and throw them out or move them or whatever. And third," Lacey went on, "my father was… Well, let's say he wasn't happy with the way things worked out when he bought this land—"

"Your brother was supposed to get the Bowen farm for the training center but he ended up getting the girl instead and marrying her," Seth Camden said with more amusement. Then, apparently to explain how he knew that, he added, "Northbridge is a small town."

"Right. Well. Just when Ian thought they could pick up the McDoogal property instead—"

"I'd already bought it."

"Yes, you had." And Lacey couldn't be sure whether that had been because the Camdens had genuinely wanted the McDoogal place or if it had been a classic Camden move.

Buying the property out from under them had put the Kincaids in a position where they had needed to deal with the Camdens rather than the cash-strapped McDoogals in order to get any land at all. They'd ended up paying more for less acreage—not the McDoogal place, but the original Camden homestead.

It was the kind of situation that Lacey had learned about in her college class, the kind of situation in which the Camdens' gain was someone else's loss.

"At any rate," Lacey went on, lifting a hand to shade her face because she thought she could feel it beginning to sunburn, "when his temper is up, my father tends to act rashly. In his hurry to get the training center underway, he didn't wait for a complete report from our people, and now we know that to build the main road leading to the center, we need access to a section of land you still own."

"And you came all the way out here today to what? Negotiate?"

"It's simple access for a road. That's all I'm asking. We can buy that strip of land from you—"

"Or lease the land for the road and pay us a fee for it in perpetuity."

Was he just thinking on his feet or was this something he'd anticipated? Again Lacey wondered about the less-flattering things that were said about Camden business practices.

"It's hot out here, so let's see if I have everything straight so you can get out of this sun," he continued. "You want to live in my guesthouse, you want me to clear out the old attic and barn, and you want to put a road through Camden land for your training center."

"Yes."

"Yes, yes and no."

"Yes, yes and no…" Lacey repeated.

"Yeah, sure, you can use my guesthouse—which does have a small kitchen, if you ever want to eat. Sure, I'll clear out the attic and the barn. But no way, here and now, am I giving the go-ahead to put a road anywhere on my property without a whole lot more information and…"

"Making sure that it's to the Camdens' advantage," Lacey muttered to herself.

"…without a whole lot more information and consideration of what all it would involve," he concluded. "At the time your father bought the property he was figuring the road that leads to the house and barn would work just fine. It isn't any of my doing if that's changed."

"It *was* your doing to buy the McDoogal place so we had to make so many changes," Lacey reminded him. She wanted him to know that she had no intention of letting a Camden get one over on her.

Seth Camden shrugged. "The McDoogal place was for sale, it connects to my place, I bought it. That's all there is to it."

And appearing innocent even when they weren't had been his great-grandfather and grandfather's trademark.

Still, Lacey knew she would get nowhere pushing him about the McDoogal place, and it was water under the bridge now, anyway. So she dropped it and concentrated on what she needed to accomplish.

"But yes, I can rent your guesthouse, and you *will* clear the attic and the barn?" she summarized.

"Absolutely."

"We should probably discuss rent," she suggested.

He shrugged again and Lacey couldn't help noticing that. Boy, oh, boy, were those nice shoulders....

Then he said, "You can just stay there. As my guest—it *is* a guesthouse, after all. Let's just consider it good relations between business associates."

Strings. That was part of what she'd learned about the early Camdens—there were always strings attached to what his forefathers did. She didn't think she could take the chance that Seth Camden might uphold the tradition.

"I'd prefer paying you," Lacey insisted.

"Okay, pay me whatever you think is fair, then. It

really makes no difference to me. Just tell me when you want to move in."

"Tomorrow evening?"

"Okay. And then we can set a time for me to come out to the old house and see what was left behind. But for now I'm not kidding—you better either get out of this sun or use some of my sunblock." He nodded toward his tools and gear at the fence.

"I'll just go," Lacey said. "But we will need to talk more about the road."

"I'm sure we can work something out," he said, as if it meant nothing to him.

They could *work something out*...

Lacey didn't respond to that. Another of the things that she'd learned in the lectures about the Camdens was that H.J. and Hank had been very big into the you-scratch-my-back-I'll-scratch-yours mentality.

After saying her goodbye, she turned to make her way back to the road where she'd parked.

"Careful!" he cautioned when she came close to falling yet again.

Lacey righted herself and glanced back to find him still standing where she'd left him, watching her.

"I'm fine," she called over her shoulder, continuing the way she'd come but taking extra care not to stumble again while he looked on.

She got all the way back to the road before she stole another glance at Seth Camden.

He was still watching her, so she waved as if to tell him she didn't require any more of his supervision and got into her car.

But she couldn't help casting another glance out into the field. Seeing him finally return to his work, she inadvertently took in the sight of that amazing backside again.

No more! she ordered herself, forcing her eyes to the road and starting her engine.

But as she drove away she was thinking about the you-scratch-my-back-I'll-scratch-yours mentality.

And wishing that she wasn't imagining scratching that back of his quite so literally.

Or quite so vividly...

Chapter Two

"Hey, Cade, it's Seth."

"Oh, man, you gotta remember that I don't keep farmer's hours," Cade complained in a gravelly voice. Seth's call had obviously awakened him.

Seth laughed. It was only 7:00 a.m. on Thursday when he called his brother in Denver. Still he couldn't resist goading him. "I thought big businessmen had to rise and shine with the sun, too."

"No meetings today—I was going to get to sleep until seven-thirty, damn you."

"Them's the breaks, pal—I had to be up two hours ago to talk to our guy running the Kentucky farm, so now I'm headed out to finish fixing a fence and figured I'd get you before I left," Seth explained.

Despite the fact that Seth was the oldest of the Camden grandchildren and so had had the option of heading the operation, he'd instead chosen to handle the Northbridge ranch and oversee all the other agricultural aspects of Camden Incorporated, leaving the CEO and chairman of the board positions to brother Cade, who was a year younger.

All of the Camdens except Seth thrived in the city, in Denver, where they'd grown up. But Seth was the country boy of the bunch by choice. When it came to the business end of things, he oversaw the farms, ranches and dairies that Camden Inc. owned. He far preferred getting his hands dirty.

"Did we lose more cattle at the Kentucky place?" Cade asked. They'd been talking frequently about a vandalism problem that had been ongoing on the Kentucky farm.

"No, actually they caught the culprits—it was just kids," Seth said. "Kids whose family owned some of the land once upon a time and decided to make a statement—you know the song."

"Somebody has an old grudge against us and they passed it down," Cade said without surprise.

"That's the one," Seth confirmed.

"What are you doing about it?"

Since the agricultural portion of Camden Inc. was Seth's baby, he made any decisions that didn't require a vote by the entire board of directors—which was comprised of himself, Cade and their other eight siblings and cousins. Petty vandalism was not a matter for the board of directors; he was merely letting Cade in on how he was handling the situation.

"The kids are locals. It's a small town like Northbridge, and I don't want any more bad blood than we already have there. I'm having them work off the damages, and if they do that there won't be any charges filed against them, so they walk away with a clean slate. The guy I have managing the farm knows the kids. He's willing to put them to work so they don't end up with a record, and we'll just hope that takes care of it."

"Sounds good," Cade said.

Seth could tell by his brother's voice and the background sounds coming through the phone that Cade had gotten out of bed and was making coffee.

"You're coming for GiGi's birthday in three weeks, right?" Cade asked.

GiGi was what they called their grandmother—short for Grandma Georgianna. She'd raised them and their cousins after the death of their parents, and she was turning seventy-five.

"Wouldn't miss it," Seth assured.

"Anything else going on there?" Cade inquired conversationally.

And just like that the image of Lacey Kincaid came to mind. That had been happening on and off since she'd left him out in the field yesterday.

"I met Morgan Kincaid's daughter," Seth informed his brother. "I'm pretty sure she thinks we bought that last piece of property just to get one over on her old man."

"Same song, different verse," Cade said.

"Yep."

They were accustomed to the distrust that came with their last name.

"Did you tell her you just wanted the property?" Cade asked.

"Nah, it wasn't an overt accusation, just an attitude—you know it when you run into it."

"I do," Cade agreed.

"Now they need a road to come through here somewhere and I think that the fact that I didn't instantly buckle under made her more suspicious. As if I somehow knew they would need to build an access road there and positioned us so we could stick it to them."

"We're a cunning lot, we Camdens," Cade said facetiously. "So she's a ballbreaker, this Lacey Kincaid?"

Seth laughed. "No, I don't think so," he said, disabusing his brother of that unpleasant notion. He didn't like hearing Lacey Kincaid referred to that way, for some reason.

"I think she would have been a match for old H.J. and Granddad," Seth went on. "Drive, determination, all business—that seemed to be what she was about. She found me clear out at the north end and hiked from the road about a quarter mile to get to me. In the heat, in a suit, in high heels."

"Just to talk about a road?"

"That and to tell me we left some stuff in the attic and the barn over at the old place. And to ask if she could stay in the guesthouse so she doesn't have to waste fifteen minutes driving to her site."

Cade laughed. "Fifteen minutes is too much?"

"According to her. I know I haven't heard the last on the road issue, but I didn't come away feeling like she was trying to squeeze me. To tell you the truth, it was more like when the girls were little and they'd play dress-up and clomp around in GiGi's heels—seems like Lacey Kincaid might be trying to fill shoes her feet aren't big enough for."

But she had been a sight to see walking away from him across that field yesterday. At first he'd simply watched to make sure she didn't break her neck on her way back to her car, but then he'd found his eyes glued to a tight, round little butt that had nearly made him drool.

Of course that had only been the frosting on the cake because nothing about the front view of her had escaped him either...

"We left things at the old place?" Cade said, pulling Seth away from his wandering thoughts.

"That's what she claims. I thought everything was out of there, but apparently not. It can't be much, though. I'll take care of it."

"And what was that about her staying in the guest-house?"

"She wants to rent it. I told her she could just use it, that I didn't care, but she's insisting on paying us something for it."

"You don't care if she stays in the guesthouse?" Cade said with an edge of suspicion to his tone. His curiosity was clearly piqued suddenly, because he added, "So somewhere between ballbreaker and little-girl-in-too-big-shoes—what's this Lacey Kincaid *really* like?"

"I only talked to her for about five minutes—just long enough for her to say what she wanted to say. I told you—she was all business. I can't tell you more than that."

"What's she look like?"

Oh yeah, Cade was suspicious, all right...

And what was Seth going to tell him? That Lacey Kincaid looked like a blonde goddess in a gray suit?

That she had hair that seemed to drink in the sun-shine and reflect it back?

That he'd never seen eyes as sparkling a green—like twin emeralds sprinkled with stardust?

That she had smooth, creamy, flawless skin and a small, perfect nose?

That she had rose-petal lips that had looked too kissable to be talking business, and high cheekbones that had flushed adorably in the heat?

That she was only about five feet four inches tall but stood straight and compact with just enough peeking from beneath her white blouse to make him have to concentrate on not looking closer?

No way was he saying any of that to his brother.

So instead he said, "Blond hair, green eyes, fills out a skirt about as well as anybody I've ever seen—she looks like any don't-mess-with-me working girl."

"Who you won't mind seeing out your back window for some time to come if you told her it was okay for her to stay in the guesthouse," Cade goaded with a laugh.

"She's not hard on the eyes, no," Seth admitted. "But she swears I won't even know she's here because she'll be spending so much time working. And I believe that."

"Too bad…"

"Nah…" Seth said, even though he recognized that there was a part of him that wouldn't hate looking out the rear of his house and seeing Lacey Kincaid.

Still, looking was all he'd do, and he told his brother why. "You know how I feel about workaholics—in the short time we had with Dad we hardly ever saw him. Toss unbridled ambition into that pot, and Charlotte brought it home for me big-time how much I don't want any part of a woman with drive, drive, drive, who puts her goals ahead of everything else and has a problem with the fact that I don't. No thanks." The thought of his ex still rankled.

"Woo, still a sore subject," Cade said more to himself

than to Seth. "Regardless, you're letting Lacey Kincaid use the guesthouse?"

"Like she said, I'll probably never see her. I'm just thinking public relations and not wanting bad blood again."

"Ah," Cade said, as if he didn't actually believe that but wasn't going to argue it.

And his brother wasn't too far off the mark in his suspicions, because even though Seth didn't want to admit it, lurking somewhere underneath everything he'd said was still a touch of eagerness to have Lacey Kincaid move in today.

But he definitely wasn't admitting it.

Instead he changed the subject to ask if Cade had gotten their grandmother a birthday gift yet.

That topic finished their early-morning conversation, yet Lacey Kincaid continued to be on Seth's mind long after he hung up.

Lacey Kincaid and all the reasons he *wouldn't* do anything more than enjoy an occasional glimpse of her from the distance.

He'd meant what he'd said to his brother—he wanted nothing to do with a workaholic or with someone who had the kind of drive he'd already seen in Lacey Kincaid.

Seth was the oldest of the kids in his family and the oldest of all the Camden grandchildren, so he'd had the most experience, and he had the most memory of his grandfather, his father and his uncle. And no memory of them *didn't* involve Camden Incorporated as their number one priority.

Yes, the intensity of their drive had built the Camden fortune. But that drive had meant that he'd had almost

no relationship with a father who had sacrificed everything to his work. It was a drive that had caused no end
of rumors that not all the means and methods used by
the Camdens were something to be proud of.

Drive that intense rolled right over other people, and
if Seth hadn't known before not to get in the way of it,
he'd had it brought home to him by the last woman he'd
had the misfortune of falling for.

So Lacey Kincaid might be lovely to look at, but
that honestly wasn't why he'd said she could use the
guesthouse. He was just being neighborly. Cultivating
good relations with the new people in town. That was
the reason.

But Lacey Kincaid was lovely to look at. And okay,
that *might* have played an infinitesimally small role in
granting her use of the place. But that still didn't mean
he was interested in her. Or that he would let himself
be interested in her.

And the fact that even at this early hour he'd already
rearranged his schedule to make sure that by the time
this day was done he would finish work good and early
so he could be showered, shaved, ready and waiting for
her when she got here?

That was just being a good host.

It was almost nine o'clock Thursday night before
Lacey arrived at the Camden ranch. After turning off
the highway she drove down a long road that ran between twin white-rail fences that bordered lush pas-
tures where horses grazed at their leisure beneath tall
oak trees.

At the far end the road circled an enormous fountain.
Water cascaded down a rock waterfall into an octagonal-

shaped pool encased in a stone wall that matched the stone of the Camden house.

The house itself was a sprawling two-story with a steeply sloped roof from which multiple chimneys rose. The windows all had earth-brown shutters, and the huge double door entrance sat atop a flight of five wide, semi-circular steps.

Lacey had first seen the place the day before when she'd come to find Seth Camden, and while she hadn't been surprised that such a place belonged to the Camdens, she had been shocked to find it in the rustic countryside of Northbridge. Among English manor houses in the hills of Wales, or mansions in the most plush, elite estates of Connecticut, maybe, but not Northbridge.

Since there had been no answer to her knocks or to her ringing of the doorbell yesterday, she didn't know what the inside of the house looked like, and she didn't have any idea where the guesthouse she'd asked to use might be or what it might be like. She'd merely been told by one of the contractors for the training center that it existed. But she doubted it was a hovel.

In fact, she thought it was probably very nice. And maybe her excitement was over getting to see her new place of residence, she told herself. Not over getting to see Seth Camden again.

Lacey went halfway around the fountain and parked directly in front of the house, turning off her engine. She left her suitcases and the rest of her belongings in her car and went up to the front door.

A lengthy moment passed after she rang the doorbell and she checked the time on her cell phone. She'd fully intended to get here earlier, but work had kept her away.

She hoped she wasn't so late that Seth had given up on her getting there at all and gone to bed.

Seth Camden in bed...

Why was she suddenly wondering what he slept in?

Then the front door opened and there he was, looking nothing at all like the Lord of the Manor.

He might not have been in a silk smoking jacket—in fact, he was wearing jeans and a simple white polo shirt—but the shirt showed hints of his muscular chest, and the short sleeves were tight around his mouth-watering biceps. The man still looked good. Really, really good...

"I was beginning to wonder if you changed your mind about this," he said in greeting.

"No, I'm sorry I didn't get here earlier and I'm so glad you're up—I was afraid you might have gone to sleep," she answered.

"Oh, I was betting that *evening* to you was going to be later rather than earlier, so I was just waiting."

Why was he betting that? And why did he sound as if the worst had been confirmed?

"I got held up in meetings and then still had a dozen things that needed to be done before I could get back to Hutch's place to load my things, and I lost track of time. When I realized how late it had gotten I thought about calling, but I didn't have a number to reach you and it seemed like I'd just be wasting more time to try to find one. But I *am* sorry," she repeated.

"No big deal. Like I said, it's what I expected. I was just doing some paperwork myself."

"Paperwork? Did you want me to sign a lease? And we didn't talk about a damage deposit," Lacey said, just in case the *paperwork* he'd been doing had something to do with her using his guesthouse.

That put a curious frown on his brow, and from there Lacey's gaze went to his hair. No hat-hair tonight, either. The deep, dark, rich brown locks were neat and clean. There was a casualness to the style, as if all it needed in the way of combing was for him to drag his fingers through it.

Sexy. It was very sexy-looking.

And Lacey reprimanded herself for that thought.

"I honestly wish you'd just be my guest and forget the whole *renting* thing," Seth Camden said.

What might she owe a Camden if she *didn't* pay rent—that was what worried her.

"No, I insist. I did some research on what it would cost to rent a small house in town and came up with an amount—tell me if you don't think it's enough…" Lacey took a check she'd already written out of the pocket of her slacks.

Shaking his head to convey his disapproval, Seth nevertheless took the check, gave it a cursory glance and said, "Fine," before he jammed it into his own jean pocket as if it were scrap paper. "And no, I don't want a lease or a damage deposit."

He gave a slight roll of those amazing blue eyes of his before he added, "Let's go through here—the guesthouse is out back. I'll show it to you and then we'll take your car around."

"Okay," Lacey agreed.

Seth stepped out of the doorway and motioned for her to come in. He was freshly shaven and smelled of a cologne that was reminiscent of the outdoors itself— woodsy and clear and crisp and clean. Lacey liked it so much she took a small, subtle deep breath as she crossed in front of him.

And then she was inside of the Camden house.

Wow! was her first thought as she went into the entryway. Lacey's father had money, and all the Kincaids lived very well. But it was nothing compared to this.

The place was as astonishing inside as it was outside. The entry was the size of a small house and reached up past the second floor to an enormous domed skylight that was like the ceiling of a planetarium, except that the stars glimmering beyond it were real.

Lacey glanced around in awe at this country mansion. Elegance and grandeur literally surrounded her in an opulent staircase that curved from one side of the entry all the way up to the second floor and swept around to the front again in the balustrade that bordered the staircase and the entire upper level.

From where she stood, Lacey could see a formal living room to the right, and a formal dining room beyond that. Straight ahead was a wide hallway with openings to the left and what she guessed was the kitchen at the opposite end.

"This place is… Wow," she said, at a loss for words. "You could probably put all of Northbridge in here."

"It's a little much for me. My great-grandfather had it built to show off. He grew up in Northbridge, got his start here. He wanted the people to know how well he'd done. I think it was an in-your-face kind of thing. I'm the only one here most of the time and I only use a handful of rooms on this floor, so the rest is just a waste unless the whole family comes out for some reason."

He didn't offer to show her any more of the place. Instead he pivoted on the heels of his cowboy boots and led her down the hallway. "I've actually considered moving out to the guesthouse myself, but my office would have to stay here so I just do, too."

Lacey stole glances into areas they passed along the way. There was a recreation room, a media room, and what she assumed was the office Seth Camden mentioned because an enormous desk was the centerpiece among shelves, file cabinets, three computer stations and various other office equipment.

"This is the kitchen," he announced, as they went into the restaurant-sized space that was well-appointed enough to excite a professional chef. But it also had a homey feel to it in the oak pedestal table and chairs that occupied an alcove, and in the six bar stools that lined the granite counter topping the U-shaped island in the center of the room.

The entire rear wall of the kitchen consisted of a series of French doors. Seth led Lacey through one of these to the outside onto a wide, covered terrace, which stood two steps above a tiled patio that was framed by lavish gardens and more tall trees.

In the far, far distance Lacey saw the three barns she'd discovered the previous day when she'd been looking for him, and an eight-bay garage. But closer in, just at the edge of the patio, was a swimming pool and a pool house. On the side of the pool was a small structure nestled in one of the stands of trees. It was single-storied and built of the same stone and in the same style as the main house, with identical windows and shutters.

"Your home away from home," he told Lacey, crossing the terrace and leading her down the steps onto the patio.

"It's so cute," Lacey said spontaneously, as she followed him around the pool to the little bungalow.

Seth opened the guesthouse door for her and flipped a switch to turn on the lights inside but waited for her to go in ahead of him.

Lacey did, entering a large, open space. A third of that space was taken up by a kitchenette complete with appliances and a round table with two chairs. The other two-thirds of the space accommodated the living room where a sofa, an easy chair, a coffee table, matching end tables and lamps faced a fireplace and an entertainment center.

"Those French doors open onto a little private patio in back," he informed her, raising his chin at the paned glass doors directly across from the front door. "The fridge has some staples in it that are yours for the using. There's coffee and tea and cereal in the pantry. The key to the lock is on the counter."

Then he pointed a thumb over his shoulder at an archway on the other side of the living room area. "There's one bedroom, one bath through there. The bedroom has a double bed, another television, and a couple of bureaus along with the closet. Sheets and towels are in the linen closet in the bathroom. You should find everything you need, but if you don't, just let me know."

And it was all spotlessly clean, which Lacey appreciated.

"It's perfect," she said truthfully. "Even more than I need."

"Great. Come on, then, we'll pull your car around to the garage and I'll help you carry stuff in."

"Oh, you don't have to play moving man—"

"Hey, if the service is good enough, I could get a big tip out of it," he joked.

Tipping a Camden—now that would be a novelty. Although the slightly flirtatious way he'd said that could mean he was expecting something other than money...

Or not. Her imagination was running away with her. And she needed to stop it!

Then Seth said, "Accept my lugging stuff in as compensation for the oversight of leaving old junk on the property we sold you."

Lacey considered arguing. But the tour had been brief, and if she convinced him not to help her, he could very well disappear into the main house and that would be the last she saw of him. So she just couldn't make herself deny his help.

They retraced their steps around the pool, through the house and out the front door, where Lacey got behind the wheel of her car and Seth slipped into the passenger side. He stretched a long arm across the back of her seat as if he'd been in her car a million times and pointed to where he wanted her to go with his other hand.

"Head a little ways farther around the fountain to that clearing in the trees—that's the drive that'll take you back to the garage."

Lacey did as he instructed without telling him that she'd done much the same thing the day before in her search for him. But when she reached the garage she refused his offer of access to one of the bays. "It's easier if I just park alongside of it—my hands and arms are usually full when I'm coming and when I'm going, and it's enough to maneuver the car door without dealing with a garage door, too."

"Sure," he said, as if that didn't surprise him, either. "But if you change your mind…"

"Thanks."

The man seemed so easygoing and laid-back. Where was that ruthlessness and relentlessness that her college professor had said marked the Camdens? That had given them such success? This guy seemed to take everything in stride.

Lacey parked and popped the trunk, and she and Seth got out of the car. It took multiple trips to unload her suitcases and two laptop computers, as well as a printer, a fax machine and several cardboard file boxes.

Seth volunteered to make the last trip alone for what remained of the file boxes while Lacey took her suitcases into the bedroom.

It was every bit as nice as the rest of the guesthouse; it had its own set of French doors that swung out onto the private patio, which was completely secluded by well-tended hedges and more shade trees.

After opening those doors to let in the cooler evening air, she went back into the living room just as Seth returned with the file boxes. He held his powerful arms straight out in front of him, biceps cut and bulging as they bore the weight of the boxes. The sight made Lacey's mouth go dry.

"Just set them down with the others. I'll organize at some point," she instructed in a quiet voice, as she tried to focus on the task and not the man performing it.

"I shut your trunk and locked your car doors— although there isn't really a need around here," he informed her as he set the boxes atop some others. Then he faced her and slid a hand into one of his front jean pockets, and Lacey's gaze just followed without thinking about where her eyes would end up.

When she realized that she was basically looking at his crotch, she yanked her head up in a hurry.

"You left these in the ignition," he said, pulling her car keys from his pocket.

He was being nice and considerate and thoughtful and conscientious, and her mind was in the gutter.

Even as she silently chastised herself, Lacey did a frantic search for something safe and bland to say to distract herself and make sure he didn't know she was thinking about him inappropriately. She settled on "So how is it that a Camden is a cowboy?"

Had that sounded sort of disapproving? She hadn't meant it that way.

Seth Camden arched one eyebrow. "Because the only jobs that matter are jobs that require suits and ties?"

So it had sounded disapproving.

"No!" Lacey was quick to respond. "It's just that the Camdens are...you know—*big business*. One of the *biggest* names in business—I even learned about your great-grandfather and grandfather in college. So I was surprised when my father said you had property in a place as small as Northbridge. And then to find you working the way you were yesterday..."

All sweaty and sun-drenched and sexy...

Lacey curbed those wandering thoughts, too. "I just didn't know that any of the Camdens *didn't* wear suits and ties on the job."

"Oh, it happens," he said, as if she were being short-sighted. But then he seemed to shrug off any offense he might have taken and answered her initial question. "We have old ties to Northbridge—"

"I remember that this is where your great-grandfather started out—"

"And where my grandmother was born and raised, where she and my grandfather met—"

"Really? Your grandmother was from Northbridge?"

"So was my mother—she met my father when he was here after he graduated high school. My grandmother converted pretty well to city girl, but my mother never did. She liked it here better, so when she was alive—and my father was busy working, which was most of the time—she would bring us kids to stay here. I guess country life just got into my blood. After we lost our folks, my grandmother would only bring us all here periodically, but it was still where I felt the most at home. So when I was old enough to make the choice, this was the life I opted for."

"Are you the hermit of the family?"

He laughed. Lacey wasn't sure whether she was relieved to hear it or if it was the sound of his laugh alone that she liked so much. But either way, she reveled in it.

"I'm not a hermit, no," he answered. "I just like country life, working the land, working with the animals. But we own over thirty farms, ranches and dairies across the country, and they're all my responsibility. I have managers at each place who report to me every day—sometimes more than once a day. I oversee things from here, then travel a few times a year for a closer look at what's going on. I keep a small plane on a strip at the Billings airport so I can get anywhere I need to be in a matter of hours if there's a problem."

Of course whatever a Camden had a hand in had to be on a grand scale. Lacey didn't know why she'd thought otherwise. Seth Camden might look like a cowboy, he might run a ranch and do the work of a cowboy, he might even have the cowboy's sense of decorum that had prompted him to help her move in, but she should have guessed that there would be more to him and to what he did than merely running a simple small-town ranch.

Before Lacey responded to what he'd said, he changed the subject.

"I think I can get out to your construction site tomorrow to take a look at what was left there. It probably won't be until late in the afternoon, so there won't be time to clear anything out, but it'll give me an idea of what's there and if I'll be able to do it all myself or if I'll need help or a dolly or a trailer or what."

"I'm not sure what you'll need, either. I do know that there's some sort of farm equipment thingy—"

He laughed. "Farm equipment *thingy?*"

"I don't know what else to call it—it's behind the barn and it looks like it hooks up to a tractor or something. But I couldn't begin to tell you what it is or what it does. So you're right that you probably need to get an idea of what there is to move before you try to do the moving."

"And tomorrow is okay?"

So she knew for sure that she'd get to see him again tomorrow...

She reminded herself once more that she shouldn't be thinking about such things.

"Tomorrow is fine," she said, as if it had no impact on her whatsoever. "Late afternoon is actually better for me because my meetings are all in the morning and early afternoon, and once the crew has left for the day I switch over to office work and that's the easiest for me to interrupt..."

That hadn't sounded good either…

"Not that you'll be an interruption. I just mean that's the best time for me to get away…"

Of course if she couldn't get away personally, there were other people who could show him what he needed to move. But somehow Lacey didn't want anyone else to do it…

"About four-thirty or five?" Seth said, not appearing to notice that she was flustered.

"Four-thirty or five is great," she agreed, deciding it might be better if she said less because every time she said more she seemed to put her foot in her mouth.

He headed for the door. "There's a landline on the wall in the kitchen—" He pointed to it. "My cell phone number and the number for my house are on a notepad next to the phone. If you need anything, just call. Try my cell first—that's the likeliest way to reach me."

"You don't have a housekeeper or staff who's over there even when you're not?" Her father had an assistant at work and a housekeeper at home who always knew how to reach him. It just seemed likely that a Camden would have at least that, too.

But something about the question made Seth Camden chuckle. "I have a lady who comes in once a week and cleans up the rooms I use. If family is due in for some reason she brings two of her friends to spruce up the whole place, but other than that everybody who works here works on the land."

Lacey nodded, realizing that again what she'd expected of him and the reality were two different things.

Seeing that his hand was on the doorknob, she said, "Thanks for the help tonight."

"Don't mention it." He opened the door to leave.

And for absolutely no reason, Lacey felt the urge to say something—anything—to keep him there even a moment longer.

So she said, "You know how to get to the site tomorrow?"

Dumb. There wasn't a single dumber thing she could have said.

Seth paused with his hand still on the doorknob to grin at her. "Uh…I do. I used to own the place, remember?"

Lacey grimaced. "Force of habit—I can't keep straight who's local and who's not, so I just automatically ask if anybody coming out to the site knows the way."

"Well, I do."

"Sure. Of course you do. I'll just see you tomorrow then."

"Right."

He stepped outside and closed the door behind him.

There was a big picture window not far from where Lacey was standing, and she instantly looked through it to watch Seth Camden walk around the pool and back to the main house.

With a cowboy's swagger that made her mouth go dry again.

Which was cause for her to command herself to look away, to put the image and every thought of the man out of her mind.

But still she went on watching until he disappeared inside the French door they'd come out of.

And as for thoughts of the man?

Even out of sight, he wasn't out of mind.

For the second night in a row.

Chapter Three

Lacey did not ordinarily go through her day watching the clock. Certainly since she'd been given the training center project, she'd been so swamped that she very often worked eighteen hours before exhaustion told her that it was well past quitting time. She'd always been shocked to realize just how late it was.

But on Friday, sitting at her desk in the original farmhouse that was being used as the construction site headquarters, she checked the time so often that it seemed as if she were aware of every minute that passed. Of how much longer it was until four-thirty. Until Seth Camden was due.

And that made her more disgusted and aggravated with herself than she'd ever been before.

What was wrong with her when it came to this guy? She was thinking about him every waking moment. She was dreaming about him when she finally could sleep.

She was picturing him in her mind's eye. Ogling him when she did see him. She'd even spent this morning looking across the pool every chance she got, while she was getting ready for work, just in case she might catch a glimpse of him.

And this was all happening now, of all times. Just when she had the kind of chance she'd strived for since she was a little girl, the chance to prove herself once and for all, the chance to be a real part of her father's love of football, the chance to actually be on Team Kincaid and prove she could handle the responsibilities her father had previously thought only to entrust to a son.

Now of all times, when the last thing she needed was the slightest distraction, not only was she distracted but that distraction was coming in the form of a man—proving her father right...

Morgan Kincaid had always relegated his daughter to the sidelines—where women belonged, in his opinion. Women, he'd said frequently, didn't belong in seats of power in the business world and especially not in the world of football. Cheerleaders. Receptionists. Secretaries. Possibly assistants. Decorators. Event planners. Morgan Kincaid had a very limited vision of the role of women anywhere. But in the Kincaid Corporation and when it came to football, those were the best positions that could be hoped for.

A woman, he insisted, would always eventually meet a man, and focus on getting him to marry her. Then, when she did succeed in marrying and having a family, that family would be more important to her than a job.

To Morgan Kincaid, that was just the way it was.

He was sexist, old-fashioned and downright silly. Lacey had argued with him again and again, citing any number of women for whom his theory didn't hold true. But her father was a stubborn, hardheaded person and there had been no telling him differently. Especially when it came to his daughter. Who he was convinced would ultimately end up a wife and mother.

Yes, Morgan Kincaid employed Lacey—after battles and battles to convince him that she wanted to work, that she could work, that she should be allowed to work. But until now, the best Lacey had accomplished within the Kincaid Corporation was to oversee the remodeling of new office space, the hiring of office and restaurant staff, discussing menus with the chefs, working in public relations and marketing.

But to play a role in any important project—particularly when it came to football? No way.

Until now.

Now, when—even though it was by default—Lacey had been given the opportunity to oversee the building of the Monarch's training center. The Monarchs—the NFL's newest expansion football team. Owned by her father. His dream come true.

But Lacey *had* gotten the job purely by default.

It was her twin older brothers who Morgan Kincaid had been convinced would carry on his legacy—both in football and in business. But long ago her brother Hutch had turned his back on the game, disappointing and alienating himself from their father because of it. Hutch had only recently returned to the family fold but not to the Kincaid Corporation—Hutch owned his own very successful chain of sporting goods stores, and it was clear he had no desire whatsoever to have anything to do with the Kincaid Corporation or working for their father.

Hutch's twin, Ian, had also had a period of alienation from the family, but had come back to the position of second-in-command at the Kincaid Corporation. Even now Ian was the chief operating officer of the Monarchs—a position he retained because he was needed there.

But as Seth had said, Ian had gotten the girl rather than the property. In the midst of acquiring the land for the training facility, Ian had met and fallen in love with Jenna Bowen. He and Jenna had ended up engaged, and Ian had been instrumental in helping her retain her family farm rather than purchasing it from her because it was the originally approved site for the training center. That had stirred Morgan's ire.

Then, to make matters worse, the McDoogal property that Ian had been confident they could get had instead been sold out from under them to the Camdens. And Morgan Kincaid had lost his second choice, as well.

Their father had been livid.

Morgan had tempered his anger enough not to out-and-out fire Ian and enter into another of the rifts that had cost him both of his sons for a while. But there had still been consequences for Ian. Morgan had punished him by taking the entire training center project away from him.

And because Morgan was determined that the project be overseen by a member of his family, by someone he was convinced had an unwavering loyalty to him, he'd reluctantly turned to Lacey. But not without letting her know that he would be watching her very, very closely.

Ian seemed to be taking his punishment in stride. He was currently far more focused on his bride and on his new life. Not only had Ian become Jenna Bowen's husband, he'd also taken on the role of father to Abby, Jenna's orphaned niece. They had adopted her as their own daughter. Ian had assured Lacey that he wasn't holding it against her that she'd been granted the project and had offered her whatever services or advice she might want.

But what Lacey wanted was to do this on her own. And to do it so well that she could finally carve out a niche for herself in the Kincaid Corporation and in her father's eyes. She'd fought tooth and nail for even small jobs on important projects in the past, and her father had left no doubt that it was only his deep desire to keep the business in the family that had garnered this opportunity for her. That this was her greatest test.

But Lacey didn't care how she'd come to have the project, and she didn't care how much pressure she was under to succeed. She was still determined to show her father that she was as much a value as his sons.

And nowhere, nowhere, nowhere in any of that did she have even a split second to be attracted to someone. She couldn't risk taking her eye off the ball.

Not even to look at Seth Camden's fabulous rear end. Or any other part of him.

This was her moment. And she couldn't blow it. She wouldn't blow it. She was going to make the Monarchs' training center a crowning jewel. She was going to do this job so well that her father would wonder why he'd ever put so much stock in his sons and discounted her.

And she was *not* going to get distracted by anything or anyone. Certainly not by a man.

Even if that man was great-looking.

It was just that thinking about Seth Camden seemed to have become second nature to her. And trying not to think about him was distracting on its own.

Those blue eyes. That slow smile. That tight backside and those thick thighs. Those massive shoulders and muscles rippling in the summer sunshine that first day, flexing under the weight of file boxes last night...

The image of him haunted her, and she just couldn't seem to shake it.

But she was going to! she swore to herself. She was going to right now!

Except that at that exact same moment she glanced at the clock in the corner of her computer screen, registered that it was nearly four-thirty and—without another thought—saved her work, put her computer on standby and headed for the bathroom.

If Seth Camden was going to be there any minute now, she had to make sure her upswept hair hadn't wilted, that her silver-white blouse wasn't too wrinkled and was still neatly tucked into her gray slacks, and that her mascara hadn't smudged. And she wanted to put on a little lip gloss...

"He'd say he was right..." she muttered to her reflection in the cloudy old mirror that hung above the rusty bathroom sink.

Her father would say he was right, that here she was, finally in a seat of power, important responsibilities bestowed upon her, and what was she doing? She was thinking about a man. She was worrying about how she looked for that man rather than working. She was suspending work in order to be with that man...

Delegate, Lacey told herself.

Someone else could show Seth Camden what his family had left in the attic and the barn. That was definitely not a job she needed to do.

But then she wouldn't get to see him...

Oh, but she hated that the thought had voiced itself.

She told herself to go with delegation. To return to the farmhouse's dining room that she was using as her office, go back to what she'd been doing—to what she should have finished hours ago except that her attention had lapsed so many times into thoughts of Seth Camden—and not so much as leave her desk to deal with him or with the issue of the things his family had left behind.

That was what she told herself all right.

But when the sound of wheels on gravel announced that someone had just driven up to the front of the house, she did a quick swipe of the lip gloss, judged her appearance satisfactory, and left that bathroom to turn toward the old house's entrance and not in the opposite direction to her office.

And when she caught her first glimpse of Seth Camden getting out of his big white truck, dressed in cowboy boots, jeans and a Western shirt, and looking even better than he did in her mind's eye?

She knew there was no way she was getting anyone else to show him around.

And she merely went outside to meet and greet him.

"As far back as when I was a kid, this place was only used for storage and for a few meetings my great-grandfather and grandfather had out here," Seth was saying as he and Lacey walked to the barn.

Meetings for some of the under-the-table deals the old-school Camdens were suspected of? Lacey wondered. But of course she didn't ask that.

She'd gone out to meet Seth at his truck the minute he'd arrived. She didn't even want anyone else to incidentally encounter him and suggest that they show him what he needed to see. Now she had him all to herself. Which made her inordinately happy…

"My brothers and sister and cousins and I all played in the barn and pretended the house was haunted," he went on. "When it sold, I came out here for the first time in about a year. There was hardly anything left and I needed to leave town on business, so I sent a couple of my guys to deal with what needed to be dealt with. I'm sorry they missed things, but now that I think of it, I didn't say anything about getting up into the attic or looking behind the barn."

"There's also a desk in what I'm told is the tackroom, too," Lacey said, as they reached the old barn. "I'm using the house as the construction office and the barn for construction supplies and equipment. I'm not really sure how anyone realized there was anything in the attic, but my crew is all over the barn and they thought the tackroom would be a good place to store screws and nails and hardware—the smaller supplies. They'll be putting up some shelves, but I don't want them to do that until the desk is out of there so I can be sure they don't damage it in case it has some value to you."

"I'll be surprised if it does, but thanks for the consideration."

There was lumber already stacked in different sections of the barn, and Lacey led the way through it to the tackroom in the rear. When they reached it, she opened the door for Seth to go in ahead of her.

And yes, when he did—even though she tried not to—her gaze dropped for a split second to his derriere. She hated herself for it, she really did. She silently berated and reprimanded and chastised herself. But still she enjoyed that glimpse of perfect male posterior.

"Yep, I remember that desk now," he said, as Lacey followed him into the room.

He took a closer look at it, hoisting one end to test the weight—probably with the thought of whether or not he could lift it himself. But when he did that the desk slid back several inches and something underneath it caught his eye.

"What do we have here?" he said, more to himself than to her.

He pushed the desk far enough out of the way to expose what appeared to be a hatch in the floorboards underneath it.

Seth hunkered down and Lacey lost herself once again in staring at his thick thighs stretching the denim of his jeans, the pure breadth of his back, the way his dark hair curved to his nape. And when his biceps bulged with the force required to pull the hatch up, chills danced along Lacey's spine.

"Buried treasure?" she said when he yanked out an old trunk from a narrow compartment under the floor, her voice cracking and giving away the fact that she was watching him rather than what he was doing.

He didn't seem to notice, though.

"Kind of looks like a pirate's treasure chest, doesn't it?" he said, setting the trunk beside the hole in the floor. "But as far as I know the Camdens have always been pretty landlocked, and this isn't big enough for *too* much treasure."

It was about the size of two shoe boxes stacked on top of each other. Hammered silver corners sealed the distressed metal that it was made of, and it was closed tight with a rusted padlock hooked through the latch.

After palming the padlock, Seth said, "Wonder where

the key to *that* is? Probably long gone. I'll have to saw it off to see what's in here."

"Gold doubloons?" Lacey suggested.

He picked the trunk up and shook it. But whatever was inside didn't sound like coins. It just made a thunking noise.

"I don't think so," Seth said. But beyond that he didn't seem overly curious as he stood again, balancing the trunk on his hip. "I might as well take this with me now and see if I can find a key that fits the lock. But the desk will have to wait. Want to show me the *farm equipment thingy?*"

He was smiling.

"It's through this other barn door," Lacey said, leading him from the tackroom through a door at the back that opened to the outside.

"Ah, that's just an old rotary hoe," Seth said the minute he saw it. "But you're right, it isn't going to be easy to get out of here. I'll need a different truck than I drove today so that I can hook up a trailer bed and haul this away."

"So another day for that, too," Lacey said, sounding cheery at that prospect. Despite the fact that she needed him to get his things moved, she was still happy to think that there would be another time when he'd come out here.

And again, she hated herself for that feeling.

"Any chance I can put off moving things until next Friday?" he asked, as they went from the barn to his truck to drop off the trunk and then on to the house for him to see what was in the attic. "The truck with the trailer hitch on it is having some work done and won't be back until then. And I'd like to do everything at once."

If she said that wasn't all right did that mean he'd have to make more than one trip?

It was tempting to find out. To see if she could get him out there twice. But that was where Lacey drew the line with herself. She was being silly and she knew it.

So she said, "Sure."

"You can let your guys start building the shelves in the tackroom—that desk is too battered already to be salvaged, so it doesn't matter if they bang it up some more before I get it out of there. I'll just use it for kindling anyway."

They'd reached the house by then. Lacey was ahead of Seth as they climbed the steps to the second floor. It didn't occur to her until they were already under way that her position in front of him put her own rear end at his eye level. It made her self-conscious and she suddenly wished she'd let him go first.

But she still hadn't thought of a way to switch places with him when they were at the foot of the four steps that led up to the attic from the second floor, so she had to take the lead on those, too. And when she stepped up into the attic itself and turned around, she caught him raising his eyes in a hurry so she knew what he'd been looking at.

But she did feel a hint of secret gratification in the fact that he had a small smile on his face.

The ceiling in the attic was high enough for them both to stand up—although Seth had to slouch as he took stock of what was there.

An old, rolled-up rug. Boxes filled with Christmas decorations, toys, books, clothing, bedding and various discards. An antique mirror. A rocking chair. And other stuck-in-storage odds and ends.

"Doesn't look like anybody got up here at all," Seth commented. "Apparently it's been overlooked for quite a while. But I'll take care of it next week."

"Or whenever," Lacey heard herself say. "We need the space in the barn, but this stuff can stay as long as the house does—which will be until construction is finished. Then we'll demolish the house and the barn, and this whole area will be practice fields—which is actually why we need a different road..."

"I saw the model downstairs. Why don't you show me what we're talking about?" Seth proposed.

Lacey was pleased with herself for having remembered the road issue in the midst of her distractions. She was only too glad to take him back downstairs where the architect's model had been put on display in the living room of the farmhouse.

She was also only too happy to talk about the training center project once they got there. To explain all that the center would encompass.

Referring to each toylike section of the model, she pointed out the administration building, and the conditioning center and training facilities that would include locker rooms, hot and cold tubs, meeting rooms, training areas, weight rooms, equipment rooms and a video department.

She told Seth about the three full-sized practice fields that were planned, one with synthetic grass, the other two with natural grass—and that one of those would be heated in order to maintain a year-round unfrozen practice field.

She showed him where the living quarters and cafeteria would be, and talked about the two racquetball courts that would be used both for training and for leisure by the team and the staff.

"But a new, more concise survey told us that the ground is flatter here, where the house and barn are—which means that it's a better place for the practice fields. The change can be easily accomplished at this stage by just turning the whole compound around to face the other direction," she concluded. "The only problem is the road into the facility. We don't want that to lead to the fields. We want it to lead to the administration building, because the administration building will be the main point of entry. It will house the visitor's area, the media room for press conferences and our trophy display area—for all the trophies the team hopefully wins."

Lacey was afraid she'd gone on longer than she should have, but since Seth didn't give any indication that he was bored, she added, "And what that all boils down to is that we need a new road that comes in off the highway right through there—" she drew the route through the model with her index finger "—which is your property..."

"I can see that," he said without committing to or refusing anything. Instead, he went from looking at the model to looking at her with interest. "So this is all your baby, huh?"

"With my father looking over my shoulder because this is the first time he's actually trusted me with anything important. But yes, it's all my project."

"What were you doing before this?"

Was he only trying to get her off the subject of the road, or was he actually curious about her?

Lacey couldn't tell for sure. Maybe it was only ego, but she thought he might actually be curious about her.

Going with that assumption, she said, "What was I doing before this? A little public relations, events planning, hiring some low-level personnel, decorating, office management."

What she didn't tell him was why she'd been given only those jobs. Then, possibly to avoid the subject, she heard herself mention something else that really was her *baby* and hers alone.

"A year and a half ago I also started a sideline of my own," she said, her voice slightly hushed, as if she shouldn't be talking about this, even though it was no secret.

"Your own football team?" he teased.

"No, but I've always wanted more involvement with the sports side of things, and it occurred to me that there are a lot of female sports fans out there. But the clothes with team logos on them are primarily aimed at male fans. So I started to design, manufacture and market a line of women's clothing using the colors and the emblems of major sports teams—some casual wear and some workout."

"Really?" Seth asked. He sounded genuinely interested.

"I've called it Lacey Kincaid Sportswear."

"How's that going?"

"It's actually taken off. I started with Internet sales— which were good—but now my brother Hutch has placed some things in his stores, and he just told me the other day when I got to town that he can't keep them on the shelves. He wants to carry my entire line, and I'm going to have to increase production to keep up."

"On top of building the Monarchs' training center?" Seth said. When he put it like that, it seemed daunting.

"I know I should probably put the clothing line on hold—of course the training center is my number one priority. But—"

"You like the clothing line." His tone of voice suggested that he could tell just how important it was to her.

"I do," she confessed. To everyone else she acted as if Lacey Kincaid Sportswear was nothing more than a hobby that had flourished. She didn't understand why she was confiding in this man now.

But she was. And she continued to. "In a way," she went on, "the training center is my father's baby—as you say. And the sportswear is mine."

"So why take this on?" Seth asked with a nod at the model of the facility. "Why not just go with the clothing line and let someone else have this headache?"

"Oh, I couldn't pass on this opportunity. I'm like a rookie player called up from the bench to show what I can do at the Super Bowl. *Nothing* could keep me from doing this. It's just that I don't want to give up the other, either."

"That makes for a very full plate."

"*Very* full. Especially if I step up production on the clothing line to meet the demands of Hutch's stores."

"But you're going to do that, right? You wouldn't want to pass up *that* opportunity, either."

"I put it into motion this morning. Between meetings for things here."

He studied her for a moment, and Lacey had no idea what was going through his mind.

Then he said, "Maybe I don't have any business saying this, but I can't help noticing that when you talk about the training center you seem kind of tense and…I don't know, like you're swimming upstream. But when you talk about your clothing line you actually smile and get into it, as if you're enjoying yourself more with that. Do you feel obligated to do the training center for your father?"

"Obligated? No! Seriously, this is the chance of a lifetime for me. The clothing line is just…for fun. It isn't as if it's important."

"Seems important to you."

"It's just a silly girl thing. Clothes. You know. But the training center—that's *huge,* and I'm lucky to get to do it."

"It *is* huge," he agreed, as if he didn't envy her the job.

"But I can handle it."

Why had she felt the need to assure him of that?

"If you say so. I'm just wondering, if it was a different situation, would you want to…?"

"Oh, I would. I do. I wouldn't pass this up for anything in the world."

Seth nodded—he seemed convinced. Then, pointing at the front door with his chin, he said, "Well, given that you are one very busy person, I probably shouldn't keep you."

It was on the tip of her tongue to tell him he could keep her all he wanted.

But she caught herself before she said it, and silently read herself the riot act for even thinking such a thing.

"We do need to discuss the road, though," she reminded him.

"I'm going to have to think about that," he said, as he headed for the door with Lacey tagging along.

"It's really only a strip of land—"

"Through one of my cornfields, which could cut down on quite a bit of yield. I'll have to do the calculations to know for sure what it would cost me."

As they went out into the late-afternoon heat and walked to his truck again Lacey persisted. "We'd be interested in buying that strip to add to what we've already purchased. So we would own the road, but you could retain the land on both sides of it." She knew that to merely lease access could get sticky in the future and become costlier than an outright sale. Not to mention that she'd learned in her class that any open-ended deal with the early Camdens had resulted in some form of takeover later on, and she didn't want to risk anything.

"We aren't in the habit of dividing our properties," Seth said.

But if the only road leading to the training center was owned by the Camdens, they could make demands under threat of cutting that road off and have the Kincaids at a disadvantage.

"Maybe you could make an exception…" Lacey said, wondering where that flirtatious tone had come from. And hating herself for it, both because that wasn't how she did business and because she should in no way be *flirting* with Seth Camden.

And yet it almost seemed to gain her some headway because it made him grin as he opened his truck door. And rather than hurrying to get into the truck, he hooked a boot heel on the runner, draped a long arm over the top of the open door and lowered those Camden blue eyes on her.

"I'll take a look at some things. Run some numbers. Study some property lines, and see what I can come up with," he said in a tone that might have had a bit of the flirt to it, too.

"I'd appreciate that," Lacey said, again more coyly than she should have.

"How much?" he countered with an attitude that told her they were venturing further and further from any sort of professionalism.

And yet she couldn't stop herself from smiling when she said, "How much would I appreciate it? A lot."

But that just made him laugh a laugh that sent ripples of something purely pleasant through her. "Are you just workin' me, *Ms.* Kincaid?"

Lacey laughed, too, because she couldn't help it. "Maybe a little," she admitted. "But I *would* be grateful."

He merely smiled at that while those blue, blue eyes of his gazed down at her as if he liked what he saw. "That might be enough," he said under his breath.

For no reason Lacey understood, her own gaze drifted from his eyes down to his mouth and she was suddenly thinking that there was an electricity between them that could easily lead to more than an exchange of banter. That could lead to kissing...

And what might it be like to be kissed by him? she found herself wondering.

Those supple lips eased into a lazy smile just then and made her wonder all the more. Made her actually wish he *would* kiss her. Just so she'd know...

Now *that* was unprofessional!

What was there about the Camden cowboy that kept getting to her?

Without an answer for that—and with even more self-rebuke just for what was going through her mind—

Lacey was the first to break eye contact. To take a step back.

"I should get to work," she said in a voice that sounded like someone who had been thinking about something they shouldn't have been.

"Sure," he answered, pivoting around to climb behind the wheel. "I'll probably see you at home," he added as he closed the door.

Lacey nodded in confirmation even though she wasn't sure it was true, since she'd looked for him so many times this morning without catching a single glimpse of him.

Still, she hoped he was right.

Then he turned the key in his ignition and put the truck into gear, casting her one final glance and raising a big hand in a wave before he drove off.

And yet even then she didn't budge. She stayed where she was, keeping her eyes trained on the plume of dust his tires left until it had settled and he was long gone.

You have a training center to build, she pointed out to herself.

And she had a booming new business of her own, too.

But there she was, watching after a truck—and a man—she couldn't see anymore.

And trying not to acknowledge the part of her that was imagining herself sitting in that truck's passenger seat, driving off with Seth Camden.

The same part of her that continued to wonder what it might be like to have him kiss her.

And itching just a little for that, too...

Chapter Four

Lacey didn't get back to the guesthouse on Friday until almost midnight. There weren't any lights on in the main house. She had no way of knowing if that meant that Seth had gone to bed, if he was sleeping elsewhere, or even if he was sleeping in his own bed but not alone—those were the unwelcome and inappropriate thoughts she'd had as she'd let herself into the small bungalow.

One way or another, she had not gotten to see him again on Friday.

On Saturday she was up at 4:30 a.m. and out the guesthouse door by five. And again there was no sign of Seth.

It was after ten o'clock Saturday night when Lacey returned to the Camden ranch, and this time as she trudged wearily from her car and past the main house, the scent of Italian food drifted out to her through the open French doors that formed the kitchen's rear wall.

Who was cooking at ten o'clock on a Saturday night?

"Hey! Are you just getting home from work?"

It was Seth Camden's voice that called to her and before Lacey could make herself look for him, she thought, *Please don't let him be over there with a date....*

"I am," she answered, turning her head in the direction of the main house.

No one was in sight except Seth. He was standing at the kitchen sink, looking at her from the window over it.

Her first impression was that he was fresh from a shower—his hair was combed back and appeared to be slightly damp, and his face had a sort of just-scrubbed look to it. He also wasn't dressed for public display—he was wearing an ancient crewneck sweatshirt with the sleeves cut off and left ragged, and—from what she could see of his waistband—a pair of extremely faded jeans.

But he could have just had an evening of crazy-wild lovemaking that had left him and his partner hungry so they'd showered, thrown on just anything and decided to fix themselves a late supper.

That was the scenario Lacey imagined in a way that both titillated her with the fantasy of herself as the partner, and tormented her with the thought that there might be another woman in that role. Another woman who just wasn't in the kitchen at that moment. Because surely a Camden—and particularly one as gorgeous as Seth—would not be spending Saturday night alone...

"Hang on a minute," he said, turning to the stove to peer into a pot before he came back to the kitchen window.

"Are you cooking? At this hour?" Lacey ventured.

"Yep. Want to eat?"

He said that so easily. Seemingly without the kind of second thoughts that were already going through her mind about why she should say no.

But Lacey had had a cold hamburger for lunch and a protein bar out of her purse for dinner. Her options inside the guesthouse were crackers or cereal. And in that instant it seemed silly not to follow his lead and just say yes.

So that's what she did.

"I would *love* to eat! It smells wonderful and I'm starving."

Oh. But what if there *was* a date somewhere on the verge of making an appearance in the kitchen...

For one instant, she'd forgotten what she'd been fretting about. She really was tired...

"My pasta water isn't boiling yet," Seth was saying. "And I just started to put a salad together—I'm about fifteen or twenty minutes away from eating if you want to make a pit stop."

Lacey had no doubt she looked like something the cat had dragged in. Which added another reason she hoped some bombshell girlfriend wasn't going to appear. But it also occurred to her that she could use fatigue to rescind her acceptance, so she said, "Are you alone in there?"

Seth made a show of glancing over his shoulder at the otherwise empty kitchen before he brought his blue eyes to her again. "Unless there's somebody here I don't know about," he said as if the question was odd.

So no date. No evening-long romp that had prompted a late supper. Just Seth.

And me....

"Do I have time for a quick shower? I'm kind of grungy," she said.

"Sure."

"Then I'll be right back," Lacey said with way more glee than she wanted there to be in her voice.

Renewed energy surged through her. She picked up speed as she rounded the pool and let herself into the guesthouse. The minute she'd closed the door behind herself she began a frantic unbuttoning of her blouse as she kicked off her shoes. Then down went her slacks to be flung onto the couch as she headed for the bathroom for the fastest shower in history.

After barely toweling off, she again opted for speed—and, taking Seth's lead, comfort, too—and put on her most comfortable undies and bra, a fresh pair of white shorts and a simple red V-neck T-shirt. Then she bent over to brush her hair from the bottom up, catching it at her crown in a rubber band, before she applied a little blush, a little mascara and some lip gloss. Then she slipped her feet into a pair of sandals and went out the guesthouse door, her fifteen-hour day a faint memory.

Seth was setting two places at one of the small poolside tables as she rounded the pool to join him.

"I was afraid I might be intruding on a date or something," Lacey said. Her two nights of wondering if he was with a woman spurred her to fish a little.

"Nope, no date. I don't do much of that, actually," he said, again as if he had no qualms about being perfectly honest.

And since that was the case, Lacey said, "So a girl-friend or a fiancée or a wife or someone isn't going to jump out of the bushes?"

"No girlfriend. No fiancée. Definitely no wife."

In other words, he was free as a bird…

Not that it mattered, Lacey told herself. She just

hadn't wanted to come face-to-face with a woman who had claim to him. She didn't want to be the third wheel.

"What about you?" he countered. "Boyfriend? Fiancé? A husband lurking somewhere while you're out here in the boonies building a training center?"

"With my schedule?" she asked with a laugh. "I couldn't keep a houseplant alive, let alone a relationship."

"You *do* work a *lot*," he said.

Lacey didn't know why, but it sounded like he didn't approve of that so she skirted around the topic. "What about you? Why are you eating so late?"

He smiled as if she'd scored some sort of point. "I was working, too. But not by choice. I had a cow that needed help calving out—"

"*Calving out*—does that mean she was giving birth?"

"It does. And she needed help. I was doing that until about an hour ago. Then I came home, cleaned up and decided to go ahead and cook what I'd been planning to cook earlier."

"So you made what's causing those fabulous smells coming from inside?"

"All by my lonesome. And with tomatoes and onions and garlic and basil that I grew."

"I'm impressed."

He grinned. "Maybe you should reserve judgment until you taste it. But you can do that now—everything's ready, I just need to bring it out. And I recommend the wine I opened—the chef has already had a glass and tells me it's pretty good."

Lacey laughed. "So you're a glass ahead of me, is that what you're saying?"

"Just one."

"A glass of wine sounds great. Let me help carry things out."

He didn't refuse the offer, so Lacey followed him into the kitchen where together they managed to collect a bottle of wine and two glasses, a bowl of pasta, another of salad, and a basket of bread.

Outside at the table once again, Seth poured the wine and encouraged Lacey to help herself to the food. One bite of the thin strings of pasta with the sauce made from fresh produce and Lacey moaned her approval.

"That's wonderful!" she marveled when she'd swallowed. "And you made this?"

He smiled. "I take it you don't cook?"

"I can't even boil water," Lacey admitted. "Many attempts were made to teach me to cook because that's what girls are *supposed* to be able to do. But growing up, I refused to cooperate with anything that came with that stipulation. It was my blanket rule and I stuck to it—if my brothers didn't have to do it, I wasn't doing it."

"Just to make a point?"

"Just to make a point."

"Hmm. I don't know if I ever refused to do anything growing up just to make a point. Or if I would have gotten away with it if I had."

"I never did much of anything that *wasn't* to make a point. And then I got older and lost that freedom—in order to have any role in the Kincaid Corporation I had to do jobs my father considered *suited* to a woman. Until now." Lacey tasted the salad of butter lettuce, tomatoes, radishes, carrots and red onions—all of which Seth said he'd also grown. It was topped off with his own secret dressing that was vinegary with an herbal accent to it.

The fact that he'd made his own salad dressing, too,

recharged Lacey's curiosity about him so she backed up the conversation a little and said, "I would be surprised if any man made this meal, but a *Camden?* Didn't you eat all of your meals with a silver spoon after they were prepared by your family's own personal chefs?"

He laughed, took a drink of his wine and said, "Oh, you haven't met my grandmother…"

"The one from Northbridge?"

"Actually, I really only knew one grandmother because my mother's parents died when I was too young to even remember them. But yeah, the one from Northbridge. We call her GiGi—her name is Georgianna, and Grandma Georgianna was a mouthful, so somewhere along the way it got shortened to GiGi. She raised us all—with the help of my great-grandfather and a husband-and-wife team who have worked for her forever. GiGi was unquestionably captain of the ship, but all four of them took care of my two brothers, Cade and Beau, my sister, January, and our cousins, Dane, Dylan, Derek, and the triplets, Lang, Lindie and Livi."

"There was a plane crash, wasn't there? That killed a big portion of your family at once?" Lacey said, recalling that from her college course.

"There was. When I was eleven. There was a trip planned for the adults—fishing for the men, shopping for the women, while the kids all stayed at home with the nannies—"

"So there *were* nannies," Lacey said. One of her assumptions of how the Camdens lived had just been confirmed.

"There were then. Before the plane crash we lived in our house with our parents, and our cousins lived in their house with their parents, and H.J.—our great-grandfather—had retired because of a heart condition and moved in with GiGi and Gramps. And Margaret and Louie—the married couple I told you about. They live above the garage. They—and Gigi, who's very hands-on—do most things or oversee what's hired out."

"And in your own houses with your own parents, there were nannies. And were there cooks and maids and butlers then, too?"

"My mother and my aunt were more into the high-society status than GiGi ever was, so yes to cooks and maids and housekeepers in our homes with our parents. But I don't remember a butler anywhere around, no."

She was teasing him and he seemed to know it—which Lacey appreciated. But the conversation was satisfying some of her curiosity about him.

"So your great-grandfather—H.J., the person who had gotten the whole Camden ball rolling—retired at one point? I thought he worked right to the end of his life?"

"Information from your college course?" he assumed. "Yes."

"H.J. had turned the running of Camden Incorporated over to Gramps, my dad and my uncle, and moved in with GiGi and Gramps about three months before the plane crash. He was still vital, just slowing down. Then, two days before everyone was set to go on the trip, H.J. fell and hurt his back. He ended up at home but in traction, and there was no way he could travel. GiGi says she didn't care about the shopping trip—if you knew her you'd understand that—so she volunteered to stay home to look after H.J.—"

"Ahh, so that's why your grandmother and H.J.

weren't on the plane," Lacey said, as she finished her meal and settled back in her chair with her wine.

"But everyone else was," Seth said solemnly.

Lacey knew from her college class that there had been suspicions that the engines on the private plane had been tampered with, possibly by one of many people who resented the Camdens because they considered themselves wronged or cheated by them.

But the crash had been so devastating that there hadn't been enough of the plane left intact to prove anything. Which some people considered fitting since the underhanded maneuvers, manipulations and machinations that H.J. and his son, Hank, were suspected of had never been proven, either.

"You were just eleven—how old were the other kids left behind?" Lacey asked quietly, sympathetically.

"I was the oldest of the grandkids. The youngest were six—my sister Jani and the triplets. The other five kids were seven, eight and nine."

"Not babies but still, little kids."

"Yep," he said sadly. "Ten scared, freaked-out, upset kids."

"I know when my mother died—Hutch and Ian were twelve, I was ten—it was awful. No amount of money or status or anything made that any better. But at least we still had our dad. I can't imagine what it would have been like to lose him, too...."

"Well, we had GiGi. And H.J. and Margaret and Louie," Seth said. "GiGi brought us all to her house, let us know that from that minute on that's where we were going to live, that she loved each and every one of us, that we were hers and that there was no question that we were going to stick together—one big family.

And that's just what we did. H.J. went back to work to stabilize the company and get people he trusted to keep things going under his supervision until we all grew up and could take over—so technically he went back to work but primarily in a supervisory role. He did his part in raising us, Margaret and Louie pitched in like surrogate parents and that was that."

"How old was your grandmother at the time, when she took this on?"

"She was fifty-five. H.J. was eighty-eight and GiGi went on looking out for him, too—making sure he ate well, that he took his medications, saw his doctors, that he didn't overdo it. Margaret and Louie were only forty, so that helped when H.J. and GiGi were a little outdated here and there—not to mention all the other ways they helped out. But we all lived in GiGi's house near the Denver Country Club in Cherry Creek. That's where H.J. died at ninety-six, overseeing Camden Incorporated until just the last few months of his life, when he had a stroke and was only lucid part of the time."

There was more sadness in Seth's tone. Lacey realized that regardless of the fact that she'd learned about the Camdens as if they were bigger-than-life, almost fictional characters, the founder of all of Camden Incorporated had just been family to Seth. His great-grandfather. One of the people who had had a hand in raising him after his parents were killed. Someone he'd loved and lost.

But after a moment of solemn silence Lacey wanted to get the conversation back to something lighter, so she said, "And your grandmother took care of her father-in-law and raised ten grandchildren without someone else to do the cooking?"

Her attempt to brighten the tone worked because Seth laughed. "*Do not* discount Margaret—together with my grandmother they could run the country. But my grandmother alone is a little bitty lady with a core of steel and some ironclad views of things. One of those views is that family takes care of family, no matter what—which is why Margaret and Louie have always been considered family and why GiGi wouldn't even think about farming us out to anyone else or so much as sending any one of us to boarding school—"

"But you must have at least been in private school, for the sake of security," Lacey said, thinking about the rumor that the Camden plane had been tampered with to cause the crash. Surely safety must have been an issue after that if not before.

"We did all go to private school, yeah," Seth confirmed. "But other than that, my grandmother did not believe in spoiling us. We made our own beds, we cleaned our own rooms, and all the other chores were revolving. My grandmother worked right alongside Margaret and Louie and we were their assistants—we dusted, mopped, vacuumed, washed walls and windows, did yard work and anything and everything else. GiGi would never ask Margaret or Louie to do a job she wasn't in there doing with them. In fact, Margaret and Louie are still there and GiGi still works with them even now, when she's about to turn seventy-five and they're into their sixties."

"And when it came to cooking?" Lacey persisted, going back to the origins of this conversation.

"When it came to the cooking there was never anyone hired to do that. GiGi and Margaret fixed breakfast— and lunch on weekends and vacations. But Margaret and Louie went home to their own house at six sharp, and, with the exception of some prep work Margaret might leave behind, dinners were just us—GiGi and H.J., while he was with us, and ten kids in the kitchen, all with jobs to do. Then we sat down to eat together and there had to be a damn good excuse for anyone to miss that," he concluded with a wide smile that told Lacey he was fond of the memories.

"I never would have guessed that was how you were raised. I think *I* was more spoiled than you were," Lacey admitted.

"Like I said, GiGi has strong opinions on things—not the least of which is how kids should grow up. And that attitude has its roots right here in Northbridge."

"She raised you all as if you were living on a farm in a small town rather than within spitting distance of the Denver Country Club?"

"She did. There's just no one like her. She's the salt of the earth, and I don't know anyone more universally loved than she is. She's practical and sensible and weathers every single storm with a stiff upper lip, a positive attitude, an eye for how things will work out for the best, and a determination to do anything she can to help—again, probably part of her small-town, everyone-lends-a-hand mentality. I've never known her not to have both feet on the ground, or heard of a problem she wasn't ready and willing to tackle—"

"After all, she took on *ten* grandchildren."

"She probably would have taken on twenty without blinking an eye."

"Am I wrong, or do you just adore her?" Lacey asked.

Seth smiled unashamedly. "We all do. Everybody who knows her does."

Seth had finished eating, too, and was lounging in his chair, his blue eyes honed in on Lacey.

"So," he said then, "nannies or no nannies for the Kincaid kids?"

"No nannies. My father also has very strong opinions about things and one of those is that a mother raises her own children—that's a woman's job along with running a household and taking care of her husband."

"But you lost your mother when you were ten."

Obviously he hadn't been simply content to talk about himself, he'd been listening to what she'd said, too.

"I did. But my father's sister—my aunt Janine—had gotten divorced just before that, and without kids or much financial means of her own, she moved in. When my dad was away—which was a lot in the football years—Janine took care of the three of us. But whenever Dad was around—or if he could manage taking the boys with him—Dad thought it was his place to make sure Ian and Hutch were raised under his influence. Janine's real job was to take over my mother's role of teaching me how to be a *lady*. But I'm not sure how successful that turned out to be..."

It had gotten very late while they'd eaten and talked, though, too late for Lacey to get into her own childhood. So she stood and began to gather dishes. "Let me help you clean up. You must be tired from playing barnyard obstetrician, and I have to be up again in a few hours so I can get to the site and finish all of my work before—"

"Your brother's wedding—it just hit me that that's tomorrow night," Seth said.

He stood, and together they got everything inside. Once they had, Lacey set their plates in the sink and turned on the water.

"You didn't go to the rehearsal dinner tonight?" Seth asked then.

"No. Hutch is marrying Issa McKendrick—"

"I know. I'm invited. I know the McKendricks well."

"Then you probably also know that it's going to be a simple wedding, with only one of Issa's sisters as maid of honor and Ian as best man, so there wasn't anything I needed to be there for to rehearse."

"Still, it's your brother's wedding," he insisted as if he couldn't imagine her missing any part of that.

"I know, but I had work to catch up on, which is also true of tomorrow. And in fact, in order for me to get finished in time for the wedding, I need to start before dawn again."

"Wow, you just never quit. I'm surprised I could tie you down for a little while tonight."

"How could I resist the smell of your cooking?" she joked, even as she thought that she could have resisted that more easily than she could have denied herself the time she'd just spent with him.

Seth reached a muscular arm in front of her and turned off the water before she'd rinsed more than their plates. "I'll take care of that, I don't want to be blamed for bags under your eyes at your brother's wedding— go get some sleep."

"You're sure? I may not be able to cook, but I'm okay at doing dishes."

"That's what the dishwasher is for."

Kitchen clean-up *would* have bought her a little while longer with him but Lacey couldn't seem to convince him that she should stay. She finally had to concede his point and head for the French doors.

Seth went with her. Lacey stepped outside while Seth leaned against the doorjamb.

She turned to face him, intending to thank him for dinner, but before she could, he distracted her a little by hooking his thumbs into his jean pockets—looking too sexy to bear.

Then he said, "If we're both going to your brother's wedding tomorrow night it seems kind of silly to take two cars. Plus I'm thinking about you being exhausted behind the wheel after working from before dawn. What do you say you let me be your chauffeur?"

"A Camden as a chauffeur?" she teased.

"At your service," he said with a humble bow of his head.

Lacey had been dreading going to the wedding alone. And while Seth *was* only suggesting a carpool, if they arrived together they might stay together...

"That would be nice," Lacey heard herself say before the *shouldn'ts* kicked in.

"Do you need to go early?"

"No, like I said, it's a pretty casual thing." Lacey wasn't sure how many people knew that her soon-to-be sister-in-law was pregnant with a baby that wasn't Hutch's. Hutch had made it clear to the family that while he might not be the biological father, he considered Issa's baby his and he wasn't in the least disturbed by the circumstances, but the information seemed like Issa and Hutch's to let out. Still, as a result of the situation, they'd decided to keep their wedding simple.

"I'm just going as one of the guests," Lacey added, "so I don't need to get there any earlier than anyone else."

"Well, the wedding is at seven—I'll be ready and

waiting for you anytime after six. Just come over and we'll go."

"Okay," Lacey said, suddenly looking forward to her brother's wedding more than she had been before. Much, much more…

But with that settled, there was nothing else to keep her so she said, "Thanks for dinner—it was really great. My compliments to the chef."

Seth grinned. "I'm glad you liked it. But everything tastes better when you have someone to eat with," he added in a voice that was quieter, his beautiful blue eyes peering thoughtfully into hers.

And suddenly, from out of nowhere, Lacey just wanted to kiss him. She wanted him to kiss her. And not in the vague way kissing had crossed her mind when they'd said goodbye at the construction site the day before. Tonight there was nothing vague about it.

In fact, the urge was strong enough for her to actually tip her chin slightly in invitation.

With Seth's shoulder still against the doorjamb he seemed to lean forward at about the same moment. Also just slightly. But enough so that Lacey thought it might actually happen. That he might actually be going to kiss her…

Until he drew back as if he'd caught himself and merely said, "Guess I'll see you tomorrow night, then."

"Tomorrow night," Lacey confirmed, hoping her extra-cheery tone concealed how let down she felt. "Thanks again for dinner." She took a deep breath and turned to walk around the swimming pool to the guesthouse, where she let herself in without a backward glance.

But once she was inside, the door closed behind her

and the lights still off, she cautiously peeked through the gap between the wall and the curtains on the window beside the door.

There Seth was, continuing to lean against that doorjamb, his gaze on the guesthouse.

And that was when she knew that she hadn't imagined anything, that he had considered kissing her.

But whether or not he'd considered it, he hadn't done it.

Should I have? she wondered.

No. She shouldn't have taken the initiative and kissed him, she told herself.

Because while she hated to admit it, there was a tiny part of her that couldn't help believing that if any kissing would ever be done, he'd have to do it.

But that was just stupid. She silently chastised that part of her that clung to the ultratraditional, sexist views she'd been raised with.

But stupid or not, that was just the way it was.

So, disappointed, she stepped away from the gap in the curtain and headed for bed.

Knowing that if Seth never kissed her, it wouldn't ever happen.

But still hoping that at some point he might.

Because for no reason she understood, it was becoming a very big deal to her that he did…

Chapter Five

The wedding of Issa McKendrick to Hutch Kincaid was held on Sunday evening in Northbridge's Town Square at the juncture of Main and South Streets. The centerpiece of the square was an octagonal-shaped, whitewashed gazebo with a steep red roof.

For the occasion of the wedding, the entire gazebo had been adorned in tiny white lights and red roses. The ceremony itself was held at the top of the five steps that led up onto the gazebo. Guests sat on white wooden folding chairs on the manicured lawn below, beneath a canopy of more tiny white lights that draped out from the gazebo's eaves like a giant umbrella over that part of the square.

Lacey had never been to a wedding quite like it. When her brother had said he and his bride-to-be wanted it simple and casual and fun, Lacey had envisioned a backyard affair like others she'd attended that had claimed to be casual. In her experience, such events were every bit as formal as any other wedding—they would be held in backyards that were more like the rear portions of an estate. White tents would be in abundance, candles, linen and silver would still adorn every table. The only really casual part of these weddings was that they were held outdoors.

But her brother's wedding was more like a friendly, small-town festival with elements of a beautiful, gracious picnic.

The brief ceremony that united Hutch in his best black suit and a veil-free Issa in a white silk Empire-waist dress with a scalloped, calf-length hem, included Hutch's two-year-old son, Ash. Ash, who was Hutch's son with his late wife, stood proudly in front of the new couple in order to be included in the nuptials that made them all a family. Dressed in his own black suit, the toddler barely fidgeted at all, but he did very solemnly parrot both his father's "I do" and Issa's, making everyone laugh.

Afterward the reception was held on the Town Square lawn underneath the canopy of lights, where round tables were set amid a border of tall oak and pine trees all lit up in more tiny white lights.

The gazebo then became the bandstand for the four-piece band, while a buffet was set out and guests helped themselves to smoked meats drenched in barbecue sauce, potato and macaroni salads, corn on the cob, and mini-cheesecakes rather than wedding cake.

"Leave it to Hutch to have some kind of country hoe-down wedding and not invite anyone who could do his business any good," Morgan Kincaid complained, as he walked up to Lacey and Seth. They'd just finished wishing the happy couple congratulations and left the receiving line.

After years of estrangement between Morgan and Hutch, father and son had reconciled in June. While tensions were lessening between them, Morgan could still be critical of Hutch. Of all of his children, actually.

Lacey knew there was no sense defending her brother. "Dad, you know Seth Camden," she said instead, fully aware that her father and Seth had met and trying to remind her father of his manners.

Morgan Kincaid instantly turned on the good-ol'-boy, football-celebrity charm and extended his hand to Seth to shake. "How are you, Seth?" the older man asked, as if they were long-lost friends.

Seth shook the outstretched hand. "I'm good, Morgan. You?"

"Great, great! Has my daughter talked to you about that little glitch with the road to the training center?"

"I told you we've been talking about it, Dad," Lacey interjected. She didn't appreciate her father interceding as if he could do a better job. Or talking business at the wedding.

"I'm looking things over," Seth assured him. "I don't see any reason why Lacey and I won't be able to come to some terms."

"Fantastic! The sooner the better," Morgan said pointedly. "And once we get this settled I'll make sure you have tickets to any Monarchs game you ever want to see—you *are* a football fan, aren't you?"

Seth shrugged apologetically. "I catch a game now and then if I don't have anything else to do, but I wouldn't say I'm much of a *fan,* no."

Lacey had to fight not to flinch. There wasn't a worse

thing Seth could have said to her father, or a faster way to turn Morgan Kincaid against him, no matter who he was. Not being a fan of the game that her father lived and breathed for was tantamount to criminal, and once he found that out, the other person ceased to exist for him. It was something Lacey had always known, but learned all over again not long ago. In a way that had struck much too close to home and might have affected her entire future if her relationship with that nonfootball fan had gone on.

Morgan Kincaid frowned as darkly as if Seth had just blatantly insulted him and turned so that his shoulder cut Seth out.

"I'll be at the site at seven sharp tomorrow morning," he said to Lacey. "You can bring me up to date on everything before the groundbreaking ceremony. You're on schedule, ready to go?"

There was nothing Lacey could do to bail Seth out, so she merely answered her father's question. "I'm on schedule for the ceremony. But our bulldozer was supposed to be here last week and didn't make it. The contractor says Thursday now, so—"

"And you let him get away with that when construction is set to start on Tuesday?"

Lacey's stomach clenched. "Things will still start on Tuesday. We just won't have a bulldozer until Thursday—"

"Which means that Thursday will be lost to unloading the thing, and it won't be in use until Friday and you'll be starting a full week late!"

"It's under control, Dad. It isn't as if everything is hinging on the bulldozer. Other things will still begin this week—materials are being delivered, other excavation can start, it'll be fine." Lacey was all too aware of her father's increasing ire and the fact that Seth was there listening.

"If you can't handle this—"

"I can handle this just fine," Lacey said firmly.

"Delays cost money, Lacey," her father said, as if that were news to her. "If you're soft you'll get run right over on this project. You have to let people know you're boss and you won't stand for screwups. If you can't do that—"

"I *am* doing that," Lacey said, forcing calm when what she really wanted to do was raise her voice.

"This isn't just fooling around, little girl. This is the NFL," Morgan Kincaid said, irking Lacey all the more by calling her *little girl*.

"You perform or you're out," he continued to rail. "That's the way it is. The way it was for me. The way it is for you when it comes to this. Don't forget what I'm trusting you with."

"I know what you're trusting me with and how important the Monarchs and this training center are to you, Dad. We'll have all day tomorrow before the groundbreaking ceremony to go over everything, and you'll see that I have it all taken care of, that I know what I'm doing."

Her father gave her the beady-eyed stare she and her brothers dreaded before he said, "I better not have made a mistake giving you this."

"You haven't."

After another dose of the stare, her father moved off to talk to other wedding guests without saying more to Lacey or Seth.

A moment of silence passed while they both watched Morgan Kincaid go. Lacey used that moment to take a deep breath and try to regain some calm, to release the tension her father almost always raised in her.

"So that's your dad, huh?" Seth said when her father was well out of earshot.

"I'm not exactly sure what to apologize for first," Lacey responded. "He gets very dismissive whenever he finds out anyone isn't a football fan. And I'm sorry you had to overhear the whole training center thing. And he didn't even say goodbye to you…"

Seth waved it away. "No big deal for me. But are you okay?"

"Oh, sure," Lacey said with some resignation. "I'm used to him. And I'm going to prove that I'm up for this job, that I can do it. When he finally sees that, hopefully he'll relax—at least a little—about letting me head this project. Then in the end, he'll have his dream training center for his dream football team, and I will have earned my stripes."

Seth nodded, but there was a sort of perplexed frown pulling at his brows. His expression made her wonder what was going through his mind.

There was no time to investigate it, however, because just then Ian joined Lacey and Seth with his new wife, Jenna, and tiny Abby in tow. Abby was dressed in an adorably frilly dress that Lacey gushed over, and since Ian and Jenna greeted both Seth and Lacey warmly, it eased the brunt of what Morgan had left them with.

It also made Lacey glad that her brother was counteracting the sour impression of her family that Seth had to have been left with.

She knew that in her father's eyes, Seth Camden was now someone to be disregarded.

And that anytime she was with him, she would be in that same category.

* * *

"7:00 a.m.—*sharp!*"

"I'll be there long before that, Dad," Lacey assured her father. He had stopped by her chair on his way out of the wedding and leaned near her ear to remind her.

It was the only contact she'd had with him since their initial conversation right after the ceremony, but still it was a relief to her to watch him go.

He'd put a damper on the evening that she'd gotten to spend with Seth. Her hope that driving together might mean that they could sort of be at the wedding together had more than been met—Seth had stayed by her side the entire evening, and no one would have guessed that he wasn't her date for the occasion. But her father had set a bad tone at the start, and Lacey hadn't been able to enjoy much of the wedding or Seth's company.

Luckily he seemed to know everyone in the small town and consequently most everyone at the wedding, and there had been no shortage of people wanting to say hello, wanting to talk to him, wanting to meet her. They hadn't actually been alone, so Lacey didn't think it was obvious that she had been preoccupied.

But now it was after eleven, other guests were also beginning to leave, and with the removal of the stress her father had caused her, Lacey felt herself deflate.

Apparently it was noticeable because just then the elderly man who had come to their table to talk to Seth left, and the instant Seth turned his attention back to Lacey he laughed and said, "I was going to see if I could persuade you to dance just once, but you look worn-out all of a sudden."

"Just what every girl wants to hear," Lacey countered with a laugh of her own.

Still, she sat up straighter and pulled back her shoulders.

She was wearing a simple navy blue sheath with a crocheted short-sleeved shrug over it. The shrug barely concealed her shoulders and was tied between her breasts to make the dress fancier, camouflaging the front of the dress in the process. But still she didn't want it to gape open due to bad posture.

And she didn't want to appear as weary as she felt. Especially when Seth was still going strong and looking fabulous in the impeccably tailored gray suit, white shirt and maroon silk tie he was wearing.

He leaned forward and said in a voice for her ears only, "You're gorgeous. You just look tired. How about if we head home?"

He made that sound so couple-ish. So caring. And it sent a warmth through Lacey that she had no business feeling.

"Would you mind?" she asked him.

"Nah. I keep farmer's hours myself. I was just waiting for you to say the word."

With that, Seth stood and pulled her chair out for her, handing her the sequined clutch purse that she'd left on the table.

"I just want to say good-night and one more congratulations to Hutch and Issa," Lacey said.

Seth stayed by her side for that, too, so Lacey was sure he heard it when Hutch said, "Don't let Dad be too hard on you. You can always tell him to take that training center and shove it, you know."

"I know," Lacey assured her brother with a laugh.

Then she and Seth said their good-nights, and Seth took her back to the sports car they'd driven here.

He held the passenger door open for her, told her to buckle up once she was in the seat, then closed the door again.

As Lacey fastened her seat belt, she watched Seth round the front of the sports car, his height and broad shoulders dwarfing the low-riding vehicle.

He slipped in behind the wheel and started the engine.

"So…" he said, backing out of the parking spot on South Street. "Your dad…I know he had to be a pretty hard-hitter on the football field, but he doesn't seem to pull any punches with you, either."

The Camden property was fairly far outside of Northbridge proper, so Lacey knew she was in for about a half-hour drive. She slipped off her shoes, angled herself slightly to the right in the seat and let her head fall against the headrest.

"He's just like that," she told Seth. She drank in the sight of his profile, knowing that she must be overly tired when she found even his ear sexy.

Of course this was just a simple car pool, nothing more, and so it was silly to even think such a thing…

"My dad didn't get where he is by being an old softy," she added. "Surely that must be true of your family, too…"

Seth cast her a smile. "When it came to business? Yeah. But I don't ever remember a time when any one of us kids was spoken to the way your father spoke to you tonight. Was he that tough on you growing up, too?"

"Oh, no. I was the little darling of the family. The baby and the girl. He was much harder on Ian and Hutch than on me. My earliest memories are of him drilling them for football, not letting up on them. But I was jealous of that," Lacey admitted with a laugh at how that sounded.

"You were the apple of your father's eye, and you were *jealous* of how hard he was on your brothers?"

"I guess it wasn't that I was jealous of how hard he was on them, but of the attention they got, of how much more important they seemed to him. He didn't just dismiss them, he took everything they were doing to heart."

"But he dismissed you?"

"With me it was always just a pat on the head and telling me I was pretty as he passed by. But the boys were his chance to keep the Kincaid legend going, to relive his glory days through them when his football career ended and they were just beginning to play. He was sure they would carry on for him in his business, too. They were *important*. It always seemed like I was adopted as my mother's consolation prize—a girl to keep her busy, to keep her company, to dress up and take shopping and have follow in *her* footsteps."

"You were adopted?" Seth asked with some surprise.

"All three of us were. Adopted and paraded out as the poster kids for adoption—it's one of my father's favorite causes. Ian and Hutch hated it, but it was the one way that I got to be included, so I was okay with it."

"You weren't *included* otherwise?"

"It wasn't as if my father ignored me, he just… Well, football, training the boys to be the next generation of football stars, building his corporation and indoctrinating them into taking that over someday, too—that was what my father was about. It always seemed as if a person only had any real value or worth or stature if they were involved in football or business pursuits with him. It's a great big boys' club. And I was The Girl. Just The Girl..."

Seth glanced at her with a grin. "Well, yeah, you are a girl," he said, approval in his voice.

Lacey laughed and delighted in that approval but didn't acknowledge it.

Instead she said, "I'm not saying that there's anything wrong with the way my father believes things should be if that's the way a woman wants it. My mother, my aunt and any number of women I know now are perfectly content and fulfilled doing what my father thinks women should do—my aunt Janine took over for my mother raising us kids and has always gone to tons of luncheons and committee meetings and charity fundraisers. She met and married one of my father's business associates five years ago, and she's really happy making a home for him, giving his parties, all of that."

"But it wasn't for you?"

"I was just so bored at fashion shows—"

"You have your own clothing line," he pointed out, finding a flaw in what she was saying.

"Not haute couture or even dresses—my stuff is sports-related. It gives women a way to *participate,* to be a part of things."

"Ah..."

"But when I was a kid, a teenager, sitting at fashion shows, going to etiquette classes, or luncheons or cotillions or being on dance committees—I felt like I was being forced into a straitjacket! Everything my father was encouraging and pushing and prodding and priming my brothers to do, that was what I wanted to do."

"You wanted to play football?" Seth asked with some amusement.

"If I could have, I would have! But it wasn't so much the playing as it was… I don't know—being denied access to what I wanted, if that makes any sense. It was like what my father was doing, what my brothers were getting to do, was more interesting, it was more of what I wanted to do than what I was *supposed* to be doing."

"Plus you felt left out…"

"As a kid, yes, I did. I *was* left out of a lot. But more than that, I just didn't want to sit on the sidelines. Okay, sure, that's where I had to stay during football games. But in every other way—in life, in the Kincaid Corporation—the sidelines were *not* where I wanted to be. And I certainly didn't want to be relegated to them for no better reason than that I wear dresses. That just didn't make any sense to me when I had the energy, the drive, the desire to be doing so much more."

Drive and desire…

There had been a hint of those things when she'd said good-night to him last night.

But Lacey didn't want to think about that. She didn't want to start thinking about kissing him again.

To start wanting him to kiss her and then have him not do it.

Again.

"So here you are," Seth said, interrupting her detoured thoughts. "Building your father's training center. Getting your chance to prove yourself."

"Finally! Yes," she confirmed. "So if my father is gruff with me, if he's putting the pressure on. I consider it my rite of passage."

"Okay," Seth said, as if he understood. "But I have to say, I'm glad I grew up a Camden and not a Kincaid. GiGi made sure we all knew that with the name and privilege came duties and responsibilities. She wanted us to be decent human beings, to give back, to do good wherever we could. But otherwise, I think we had it a lot easier than you all did. I know no one felt any more or less included or important—or as if they had to prove themselves—because they were born male or female. And I also know that if I'd been at the wedding of one of my brothers or my sister or one of my cousins tonight, we would have been drinking and dancing and toasting, and no one would've been riding anyone else about work."

"Dad just wants to be sure that everything is perfect. I understand that," Lacey said in her father's defense. "And I told you, this is my chance."

They'd reached the Camden ranch by then and as Seth pulled around the house and into one of the slots in the garage, he said, "I guess that explains why you're so happy to be working eighteen-hour days."

"Are you keeping tabs on me?" she challenged more flirtatiously than she'd meant to.

He shrugged, and her gaze rode along on those big, broad shoulders before she glanced at the smile that said she'd caught him at something.

"I wouldn't say I'm keeping *tabs* on you, no. But I've noticed when you're around or coming or going. When you're not around…"

Lacey never came or went or passed by a window in the guesthouse without glancing at the main house hoping for a glimpse of him. And there were innumerable times when she was home when she made a special trip to a window to look across the pool, too. Now she wondered if he was doing the same thing from his vantage point. Because it sounded like that might be the case.

She hid the satisfaction that gave her by finding her shoes on the car floor and putting them back on as she said, "Yes, I am happy to be working eighteen-hour days. Or more if I need to. I'll do whatever it takes."

"That's something I've heard before," he muttered to himself, as he turned off the ignition and got out.

Lacey didn't wait for him to come around. She let herself out and met him at the trunk of the car.

She wasn't sure what his muttering had meant but the way he'd said it didn't sound altogether favorable so she opted to let it go. Instead, as they walked out of the garage together, she said, "Will I see you at the ground-breaking tomorrow?"

"Rumor is it'll be quite a spread," Seth answered.

"Dad wants the whole town to be excited about Northbridge being home to the Monarchs. The team and all the trainers and coaches and staff are coming, and with an open invitation to the town, we're expecting quite a turnout. After the ceremony there'll be food and drinks, and the model will be on display under its own tent where everyone can see the layout and the way it will all look. It seems only fitting that you should see the groundbreaking on the ground that used to be yours."

Not to mention that she really wanted him to be there just for her sake, that getting to see him in the process of doing her job somehow didn't seem as taboo as she kept telling herself things like tonight were.

"It's tomorrow evening?" Seth asked.

"Six o'clock. We wanted it to be at a time that wouldn't interfere with anyone's work—again, so more people would come."

"My day should be wrapped up by then, so yeah, I'll probably be there."

Not much of a commitment. He'd said it almost as if there was a part of him that was reluctant.

"Maybe you don't want to see the first step of your family's farm turned into something else," she said.

"No, I'm fine with that," he said.

She was confused as to why he might have dragged his feet. But she didn't pursue it. He'd said he would come and that was what mattered.

Lacey wasn't sure why, but he'd gone with her to the guesthouse door rather than parting ways when they'd reached the pool and going to the main house himself.

But in keeping with how the rest of the evening had seemed, it was very much as if he'd walked her to her door after a date. And it was on the tip of her tongue to invite him in…

Which of course she wasn't going to let herself do.

Even though she secretly wanted to…

What she did was unlock the door, open it and take a single step inside before she turned to face Seth.

"Thanks for tonight," she said. "For driving and for keeping me company through everything. It was nice having an insider to introduce everyone and fill me in on who was who."

"No thanks necessary. I enjoyed myself. Even if I never did get you to dance."

"I hated cotillions, remember?" she said.

But the truth was that she'd avoided dancing with him despite wanting to more than he could know. She'd been too afraid all evening of finding herself in his arms. Of using that opportunity to hold on tighter to him than she should. Of resting her head on his chest. Of moving in close and pressing herself to him. Of doing any of the things that would have given away to her father that she was attracted to this man. That would have made her father think that he shouldn't have given her the training center project because she was going to prove him right and put a man before her work.

"You could have danced with someone else," she told Seth. She hadn't suggested that, though, because he actually might have taken her up on it.

"I didn't want to dance with anyone else," he said then, his deep voice quiet, a small smile beaming down at her as his blue eyes peered into hers.

"Maybe next time," Lacey heard herself say wistfully, thinking that if only there could be a next time. *Without* her father around...

"I'll see you tomorrow, though?" she added then.

"You will," he confirmed.

But that was all he did. He didn't add a good-night. He didn't move from where he was standing tall and handsome in that dashing gray suit, looking nothing like a small-town rancher. He merely went on gazing down at her, studying her.

And yes, kissing was on Lacey's mind once more. On her mind and making every ounce of her long for it.

But she wouldn't be the one to kiss him first. She wouldn't. No matter how much she wanted to...

Then Seth reached a hand to either side of the door frame to brace his weight and leaned in across the threshold to do exactly what she wanted—to kiss her.

But too fast!

Almost before she saw it coming, before she could respond, before she could even close her eyes, it was over...

Fleetingly, she considered taking it from there and

dealing out a second kiss herself. A longer, more lingering, better kiss that she could actually savor.

But she didn't do that.

She just tipped her chin a little to let him know she wouldn't hate it if he did it again.

Only he didn't.

He just said a simple good-night, pushed off the door frame, turned and headed for the house.

Lacey shut the door and closed her eyes for a moment, trying to relive that kiss, barely recalling the feel of his warm, supple lips. The scent of his cologne. His breath against her cheek…

He'd kissed her.

He *had* kissed her!

So it wasn't just a one-way attraction…

She opened her eyes, and there in the darkness of the guesthouse she smiled a secret smile.

Because while she knew this shouldn't be happening, while she didn't have the time or energy for it to happen, while she needed to put everything she had into the training center project and into proving herself to her father, while tonight she'd also seen for herself that Seth didn't fit in with her family—the same disastrous way that way Dominic hadn't—Seth *had* kissed her.

And something a little giddy went off inside of her just knowing that he'd wanted to.

That he was looking every day and night for signs of her the way she was looking for signs of him.

That he'd given in at the end and kissed her.

And no matter how brief that kiss had been, it had still been a kiss.

Chapter Six

Lacey Kincaid was a dynamo.

That was what Seth thought repeatedly throughout the groundbreaking ceremony on Monday evening.

The ceremony itself was held under a circus-sized white tent with a podium at one end, tables laden with food and drinks along the sides. Attendees filled the rest of the space.

For Seth it was almost impossible to concentrate on Morgan Kincaid's speech, on Morgan Kincaid introducing each member of the Monarchs team and staff, on the mayor's welcome-to-Northbridge speech and the Monarchs-as-a-boon-to-Northbridge talk that the head of the City Council gave. He didn't even spare more than a glance at the Monarchs cheerleaders when they performed.

But he was aware of where Lacey was every moment, of her every movement.

It was clear to him that she was orchestrating and overseeing the entire event despite the fact that after introducing her father at the start, she never took center stage again. But from the background she directed speakers on and off the podium, and made sure there was smooth transition from the speeches to the introductions to the entertainment. She also began the applause at the appropriate moments, encouraging it from the large crowd that had come out for the event, and deftly quieting it when it was time for whatever or whoever was next on the program.

Sometimes, when Seth was watching her, she slipped away, behind the rear curtain of the tent that kept them all out of the August sun. But she was always gone only for a moment before she returned.

And he was always glad when she did. For no reason he could figure out.

She repeatedly checked the clipboard she had with her, spoke into what appeared to be a walkie-talkie and was quietly consulted several times by other people sidling up behind her to whisper in her ear. But to anyone who wasn't paying particular attention to Lacey, it all appeared to be Morgan Kincaid's show—he was the star, he was the host, and he was the one who dug out the first shovelful of earth when that rear curtain was dramatically lifted and he stepped off the podium to actually break ground amid cheers that Lacey instigated.

At the meet and greet that followed the ceremony, Seth sauntered around. He socialized with other townsfolk, but never without a portion of his attention on Lacey. He tried not to be transfixed by her, but no matter where he was or who he was with, he was still watching her bustle around, tending to everything, seeming to be in her element juggling half a dozen things at once and keeping up a hectic pace to do it.

The longer things went on, the more he realized that he wasn't likely to be able to rein her in and get even a few minutes alone with her. Yet he still couldn't keep his eyes off of her.

She was dressed much like she'd been that first day they'd met, when she'd found him out fixing the fence—blue-gray, pencil-skirted business suit with a conservative white blouse underneath the jacket, and three-inch-high heeled pumps.

Her shiny, pale blond hair was pulled into a twist at the back of her head with some curly ends sprouting out the top at her crown. Her cheeks were pink, her eyes were bright and her lips...

He'd kissed those lips on Sunday night—he couldn't stop thinking about that—and every time he looked at her, he just wanted to kiss them again....

Which he told himself over and over was a damned dumb thing to keep thinking because he couldn't even catch up with her to say hello.

And he knew from experience that that was the way it was with dynamos.

High-energy, ambitious, determined, single-minded, driven—not only had Lacey described herself in those terms, Seth recognized it in her. Especially when he saw her in her element at the groundbreaking. She was a whirlwind.

And that wasn't him. It wasn't *for* him.

He liked small-town country living, farming and ranching, specifically because it allowed him the pace *he* thrived on. Sure, the work he did was hard—sometimes backbreaking—and it took time and required a seven-day-a-week schedule and frequent predawn days and even late-night hours if he had a sick animal or a storm to gauge or any number of other things that could happen.

But there wasn't the kind of pressure, the kind of demands and anxiety and competitiveness that went with the corporate world, the business world.

The kinds of things that Lacey seemed to thrive on.

Not that there was anything wrong with what it took for either of them to flourish and be happy, to meet their goals. It just made them two very different people who wanted very different things, who lived very different lives.

And when things—people—didn't mesh, they didn't mesh. He knew from experience that he would take a backseat to the kind of drive and determination that fueled Lacey. And worse still, that she could want and expect him to change.

Given that, he told himself, he should stop dragging his heels and go home. He should stop standing around hoping that Lacey might find a minute to do more than cast him the few glances, the small smiles, the scant waves she'd cast him throughout this evening.

That's as good as it's gonna get, he thought. He should just give up the ghost and go.

Finally listening to himself, he wove through the crowd to get to the buffet table and set down the lemonade he'd been nursing. He decided along the way that he wasn't even going to make an attempt to say goodbye to Lacey, that he was just going to leave.

And that was when he saw her excuse herself from talking to a group of football players and—keeping her

green eyes honed on him to the exclusion of all else—
she crossed to Seth.

"Can I ask a favor of you?" she said when she reached
him, not seeming to realize there was no greeting in
that.

"Anything," Seth answered. He could have kicked
himself for how grateful he was that she was finally
paying some attention to him, for the fact that the hours
he'd spent at this event hoping for a little time with her
suddenly seemed like less of a big deal now that she
was standing right there in front of him.

"It looked like you might be ready to take off—"

"I was."

"I haven't had time for a single bite of food today,"
she continued. "And that isn't going to change while
this is going on. If I ask the caterer to pack some of this
before everything is gone, would you take it home with
you so I'll have something to eat when I get there?"

I should have known...

But apparently he'd been hoping that she was going
to ask him not to go because disappointment flooded
him when she didn't.

Still, he said, "Sure," chafing at the fact that now that
she'd finally sought him out there still wasn't anything
personal being exchanged between them, that she was
only engaging him because she'd thought of how he
could be of service to her.

Because that's what backseats were good for...

"Thank you *so* much!" she said, as if he'd rescued
her.

"Sure," he repeated with an edge he couldn't keep
completely out of his voice. This felt much too much
like déjà vu to him, too much like times with Charlotte.

"Lacey!" her father called to her from the other side of the tent, motioning with one hand for her to come.

"I'm sorry I don't have time to talk. But I really appreciate this!" she said then, dashing away without delay after giving the caterer his instructions.

And just like that Seth was alone and watching her from a distance again as she jumped back in.

"Can you pack that food up now?" he asked the caterer. "I'm done here."

And in that moment when he said it, he was thinking that he was finished with more than the groundbreaking event. That he was also finished with letting himself be in the grip of this attraction to Lacey.

And he meant it.

Until he had the food he'd agreed to take with him and he was on his way out of the tent.

Because that was when Lacey's eyes locked on him once more and she smiled a smile that seemed to be for him alone.

A smile that made everyone else around them, everyone that separated them, seem to fade away.

A smile that drew his gaze to those lips once more.

Those lips he'd kissed.

And despite everything, despite his best intentions—and hating himself for it—he still just wanted to kiss her again…

It was after ten o'clock when Lacey's day ended and she finally returned to the Camden guesthouse.

Lights were on in the main house—she never failed to notice that whenever she was coming or going—but there was no sign of Seth.

She soon discovered that he'd left the food she'd

asked him to bring home for her in the guesthouse's refrigerator. She was dizzy with hunger.

But the guesthouse seemed stuffy, so she opened windows, kicked off her shoes, tossed her jacket over the arm of the sofa, and went barefoot—food containers, a napkin, a glass of water, and a fork in hand—back out to eat at one of the half-dozen poolside tables.

Another glance at the main house told her nothing had changed—Seth was still nowhere to be seen. She faced in that direction anyway, sitting down to eat but keeping the French doors in her peripheral vision.

The containers held finger sandwiches, pulled pork glistening with barbecue sauce, tiny hot dogs wrapped in puff pastry, and pinwheels of flour tortillas rolled like jelly rolls around refried beans, guacamole, peppers, olives and cheese.

Lacey was so hungry she didn't know where to start. She popped one of the pinwheels into her mouth, then jabbed her fork into the pork with one hand and picked up a hot dog with the other.

And of course, just when she was the picture of gluttony, Seth appeared in the main house's kitchen and caught sight of her.

She could see through the French doors that he was barefoot, too.

Lacey didn't know why that was the first thing she noticed about him, but it was. Barefoot but dressed in faded jeans and a plain white T-shirt, his dark hair only finger-combed but looking sexily disheveled, his face beginning to show the faint shadow of beard.

When he saw her he hesitated, and Lacey had the impression that he was tempted to do nothing more than a neighborly wave before going on about his business.

But then he came as far as the French doors, opening a single set of them and stepping only to the threshold, where he leaned against the frame. He seemed intent on staying there, since he crossed one leg over the other and both arms over his chest. Keeping his distance, maybe…

"Another long day, another late night," he said, somehow sounding disapproving of that.

"I'm glad it's over!" Lacey responded after swallowing her food. But she was too hungry to resist the bite of barbecue before she held the hot dog aloft and said, "I'll share if you're feeling like a snack…"

What she really wanted was for him to stop keeping his distance and come closer, to join her.

"Not hungry," he answered, staying where he was and giving her the sense that he was purposely being standoffish.

"I kept hoping I'd get to talk to you at the groundbreaking—I'm sorry that didn't happen," she said, not because she thought it mattered to him. She'd seen him chatting and mingling and fitting right in with his fellow townsfolk, and she doubted that he'd missed her the way she'd missed having even a moment with him. "It looked like you were pretty well occupied, though."

"I was hoping I'd get to see a little of you, too," he said.

"How about now?"

The invitation went out purely as a reflex because she just wanted him to come and sit with her, to give her those few minutes she hadn't gotten to spend with him earlier.

But he didn't instantly accept the invitation. Instead he seemed to ponder it, not appearing eager to oblige her.

Then, almost reluctantly, he finally shoved off the

doorjamb and came with a leisurely cowboy swagger around the pool to her table.

Lacey was just happy to have him there and couldn't help a small smile between bites of hot dog, more barbecue and another pinwheel.

"You saved my life with this food," she told him, as he sat on the chair across from her. "At home there are a dozen fast-food places I could choose from even late into the night, but things aren't that way in Northbridge. And I had to take care of everything else at the groundbreaking—there was no way to take care of me, too."

"You were running around."

"Like a crazy person! I was thinking that once the ceremony was over and people were just eating and drinking and talking, I could take some time for myself. I thought I'd maybe see if you wanted to sneak away with me and a couple of plates of food so I could just have a breather." She confessed this a bit quietly because she wasn't sure that was something he would have been interested in, and she didn't want to presume anything.

"That would have been nice. I would have liked it," Seth said, still with some reserve.

"But there was just no way. Every time I'd get a bead on you, say 'Excuse me' and take a step, someone or something else would have to be dealt with. And then I saw you set down that glass and I just knew you were leaving before I'd even gotten to say hello…"

"So you figured the next-best thing was to enlist me to bring home food?"

There was still something in his tone that said he wasn't particularly happy with her, but she didn't understand it. She pretended she hadn't heard it and said, "Definitely not the *next*-best thing, but I was desperate. And if you'd just have something to eat so I'm not the only one of us stuffing my face, this is *sort* of what I was aiming for earlier...."

He studied her for a moment, and Lacey thought that he was choosing whether or not to go on being stiff and standoffish with her. She still wasn't sure what was going on with him.

But then he shook his head as if in concession, sighed, took one of the pinwheels and popped it into his mouth.

He also sat slightly lower and more comfortably in the wrought-iron chair before he said, "Where *is* home for you when you aren't here—the place with all the fast-food restaurants you could want? I know your father is based out of Billings—he told me that at the closing on the land. But what about you?"

"I live in Billings, too. Where I grew up. In the carriage house at my dad's, actually."

"You still live with your father?"

"The carriage house is separate," Lacey explained. "And farther away from my dad's house than the guesthouse is from you. Plus it faces away from his house, so my front door is on the block behind his. We never know when the other has company or is coming or going or anything. I have to go out my back door and across tennis courts and his whole backyard just to get to the rear entrance of his place."

But yes, she *was* defensive about it because it sounded as if she'd never left the nest.

Which was why she added, "I lived at college for four years, shared an apartment with a girlfriend after that, then lived with someone else for two years—until two years ago—but then it was...I don't know...less lonely to go back home than to get an apartment or a house by myself."

"The *someone else* you lived with was a guy? A husband?"

"A fiancé. I've never been married," she said, unwilling to say more, so she went in another direction. "By then my friends from high school and college were all married and having kids. Almost everyone I work with is male except for the few women secretaries or assistants—and they don't relax around me enough to be friendly or to make friends outside of work—so I was really pretty isolated. The carriage house seemed like a way to maintain my independence but still not be as cut off as I felt at the time."

"And I'm betting that in the two years since you moved into your father's carriage house you've been too busy to make any new friends."

Busy—that word had an edge when he said it, but Lacey wasn't quite sure why, so again she ignored it.

"I have been too busy. Especially since that's about the time I started to work on my clothing line. Since then I've basically had two jobs."

"And now you have the biggest job yet."

"And now I have the biggest job yet," she confirmed.

"So no personal life? No social life?" he asked, frowning a bit at her.

"Not really. I get the occasional invitation but I usually have to turn it down unless it's for business. And I haven't had time for dating—so no, not much personal life or socializing."

"What about hobbies? Don't tell me work is all you ever do."

Lacey shrugged. "Okay, I won't tell you that, but it's the truth."

"How about movies or TV or skiing or sailing or hiking or knitting or gardening or…I don't know—kickboxing. Isn't there something you do to wind down?"

Lacey laughed. "Winding down—now that's a trick I haven't mastered. Tonight, for instance, I'm tired but I'll still have trouble sleeping—"

Of course Seth was part of that problem lately because she couldn't stop thinking about him. Thinking about what they'd talked about or done. Thinking about him being just a few yards away. Thinking about what he might be doing or if he was sleeping—and what he might be wearing if he was. Thinking about that kiss last night…

"And while I'm having trouble sleeping, it seems like a waste of time not to bring a little paperwork to bed with me, so I guess you could say that that's what I do to wind down—paperwork in bed."

Seth shook his head again. He let his blue eyes bore into her for a long moment, his expression showing disbelief.

Then he sat forward and said, "Are you done eating?"

She'd been eating all along, but had definitely slowed down. "One more thing…" she said, peering into the containers until she found the small cup of butter mints she'd asked for.

She offered them to Seth.

He took two and popped them into his mouth. She did the same.

"Okay, now I'm done."

Seth stood and began to gather the food containers as he gave instructions. "Go inside and change your clothes. Put on something old and comfortable that can be washed. And shoes that can get dirty. I'll throw this stuff away, get some shoes myself and meet you back here in a few minutes."

"For?"

"I'll show you one of the things *I* do to wind down."

The thoughts that went through her mind when he said that shocked her. It didn't involve a change of clothes; it involved *no* clothes...

There was just something about this guy that brought out a randy side of her that she hadn't even known she had.

She might not have taken his orders except that the standoffishness he'd been exhibiting before was gone and she was so glad that she didn't want to rock the boat. Plus she was curious about what he had up his sleeve and—as always—she was enjoying being with him and didn't want it to end.

Still, she said, "Am I going to hate this?"

"Maybe," he answered with some orneriness.

But then he took her food containers around the pool with him and headed inside of his house. "Go on, change," he called over his shoulder.

Lacey gave him a mock-stern look.

But, smiling to herself, she pivoted on her bare heels and did as she was told.

Twenty minutes later, dressed in a pair of old jeans and a T-shirt, with her most worn-out tennis shoes on her feet, Lacey found herself being led to one of the three warehouselike, state-of-the-art, two-story barns behind the garage. A place where she assumed animals were housed.

"I'm not crazy about getting too close to pets that are bigger than I am—if that's how you're thinking to get me to relax, it might not be the best idea," she warned, as Seth led her inside.

He merely smiled.

The structure was dimly lit until he flipped a switch, and then it was flooded with bright light. Lacey could see a horse looking out one of the stalls in the distance to the right of a wide center aisle. That was the only animal in sight.

"That's Bud, but he's not who we came to see," Seth informed her. "We're here for Bud's wife, Milly. She's a sweetheart. I brought an offer of friendship that will win her over, so there's nothing for you to be nervous about."

Lacey had noticed that Seth was carrying an apple, but she'd thought maybe he was going to eat it himself.

"It's a little smelly in here," she observed, peering into empty stall after empty stall as they went up the center aisle.

"Smells like a barn. Since most of the animals are out in the paddocks, this is nothing."

As they reached Bud's stall, the big, black horse raised his head as if in greeting, and Seth patted his nose.

"Sorry to bother you, Bud," he apologized, pausing to take what appeared to be sugar cubes out of his pocket with his free hand and feeding them to the horse before they moved on to the next stall.

As they approached it, he said, "Milly, you have company."

A brown face with a white blaze down the nose appeared over the stall's half door in answer.

"Bud's wife, Milly?" Lacey asked with a laugh.

"Milly and Bud are my oldest horses—they've been here since we were all foals—after a lot of begging, my grandfather made them my seventh birthday present. They were a few months short of turning one. They were bought together, and they've been inseparable ever since."

"That's why they're the only two horses in here?" Lacey asked.

"They're fairly old for horses, and they don't do as well in the high heat or the coldest cold, so they spend a lot of time in the barn year-round, where it's climate-controlled. Bud can be a little more cantankerous, but Milly is as gentle a horse as I've ever known."

Seth handed Lacey the apple. "Just hold it out to her in the palm of your hand. She'll take it."

"And my hand with it?" Lacey asked, only half joking.

"Maybe just a finger or two," Seth said, grinning and obviously enjoying his own humor.

Lacey did as he'd instructed, holding the apple in the palm of her hand and tentatively offering it to the horse.

The animal took the fruit without Lacey feeling anything.

"Now rub her nose like this—" Seth demonstrated and Lacey followed suit.

"Okay, I'm relaxed already," she announced, implying this outing didn't need to go any further.

Seth chuckled at her and opened the stall door. "Stay with me to the side of her and keep a hand on her shoulder or her back so she knows you're there."

Again Lacey did as she was told and followed him into the stall.

"Milly loves to be brushed," he said, taking a brush

from a bucket nearby. "Sometimes I think she almost purrs, she loves it so much, and if you let yourself, you start to feel as good about it as she does. This is how you do it."

Once more he demonstrated, showing Lacey how to smooth the brush over the horse's coat in the direction that the hair grew; how to take slow, soft, rhythmic strokes; advising her to clear her mind and just be at one with the animal and the simple task of grooming her.

Then he handed the brush to Lacey.

She again did what he'd showed her, and strangely enough she could feel how much the horse really did like the brushing. The animal seemed to almost lean slightly into each stroke, and several times she turned her head to that side as if to tell Lacey how much she liked it.

And yes, Lacey did find the repetitive motion surprisingly soothing. Although in truth she thought it had more to do with Seth standing so close by, his big body protectively hovering, his powerful hand resting on the horse's hindquarter as if to make sure Milly knew who was boss.

There was something comforting and arousing at the same time in his mere presence there. In his commanding, take-charge attitude. In how strong and capable he was. In his ability to be master to the huge animal.

"Okay, you're right, there *is* something about this that kind of lulls you—smells and all," she said.

Seth grinned down at her. "Don't insult Milly by saying she stinks."

Lacey laughed. "Sorry, Milly," she said without taking her eyes off of Seth.

Lacey brought the brush to a stop on the horse's back, not far from Seth's hand, and laid her own head atop her outstretched arm as if she were too tired to go on. "Maybe I should just sleep out here in the barn," she joked.

"Bud would get jealous," Seth said. "He shares Milly for a little grooming but that's about all."

"He's possessive…"

"Well, she does seem to belong to him and he really likes her. You can't blame a guy for that…."

Lacey had the impression that Seth wasn't talking about the horses alone. That just maybe he was talking about himself. Liking her…

She was just glad to be there with him. To be looking up into that oh-so-handsome, slightly scruffy face. Into those blue eyes that were peering into hers in a way that let her know that all the stiffness, all the standoffishness that she'd sensed in him earlier was gone. A way that reminded her of how he'd looked at her just before he'd kissed her the night before…

Then he leaned forward. Instinct brought Lacey's head up off her arm to meet him in a kiss.

Tonight it wasn't over in a flash.

No, tonight's kiss allowed their lips to meet lightly at first, then more firmly. It went on long enough for eyes to close and heads to tilt, naturally deepening all on its own.

It was a kiss that mingled his sweet breath with hers and let her know the full feel of his warm, supple, agile lips accompanied by just the slightest roughness of that shadow of his beard. The slightest roughness that she kind of liked…

Apparently, Milly didn't like being the leaning post that supported their kiss, because the horse whinnied and nudged at them to let them know she was still there.

And ended the kiss before Lacey was ready to have it end.

Long before...

But Seth broke away to stand straight again, leaving Lacey no choice but to do the same.

Seth translated Milly's neigh and nudge. "If there's nothing in it for her, we're just bothering her."

"I think I've sufficiently learned the value of brushing a horse," Lacey said, unwilling to go back to the chore when they'd moved on to something she liked so much better.

Seth took the brush from her and patted the horse's rump once before dropping the brush back into the bucket and motioning for Lacey to lead the way out of the stall.

"'Night, Milly. 'Night, Bud. You two sleep tight," Seth advised the horses as he and Lacey retraced their steps to the door. He turned the lights down to a dim glow again as they left the barn.

Lacey had to admit to herself that whatever happened in that barn *had* left her feeling more relaxed, though. More at peace. More uplifted. But whether it had been the horse brushing or the kiss was a question she wasn't sure she should answer.

"It *is* nice out here," she said as they walked back to the pool area, feeling under the influence of the night air. "Peaceful, quiet and clean-smelling."

That made him laugh. "Nothing like a little barn perfume to make you appreciate fresh air."

She was hoping that once they reached the pool they wouldn't split to go their separate ways. And they didn't—Seth walked with her to the guesthouse.

But that was all he did before he said, "Now you

can shower off the horse hair and smell and go right to sleep—works for me every time."

"I *will* welcome the shower," Lacey said, even though she hadn't had enough to do with Milly to really need it.

Seth merely smiled down at her for a moment before he did what she wanted him to do—kissed her again. Another kiss that went on just long enough for her to be getting into it before it ended, even without the horse to interrupt them.

Then Seth said a simple good-night and left her. She went into the guesthouse and closed the door behind her, then stood there staring at it.

Staring at it and thinking about what she could do if only she didn't have to rush to bed in order to get up again before dawn and be at work hours ahead of the earliest of her construction crew.

Thinking about going back outside, suggesting to Seth that they open a bottle of wine to share.

Thinking about where the rest of the night might take them, if only she could let it.

She yearned for that so much that it was a fight not to give in.

But she didn't. Instead she reminded herself of all she had to do the next day.

And once again went the way of her goals.

Chapter Seven

The first week of construction on the training center did not go well. In fact it was hellish for Lacey. Equipment still hadn't arrived. The wrong materials were delivered, had to be returned, reordered, and replacements were delayed. Her contractor had a family emergency and had to leave the state. Her construction foreman broke his wrist. A midweek windstorm blew down a power line.

To Lacey it seemed as if anything that could go wrong had. Plus she'd had problems with the fabric being used to make the bike shorts in her clothing line, there was a sudden increase in orders for hoodies that she wasn't sure she could meet, and three new vendors had gotten irate over a shipment mix-up.

By Friday she was exhausted from getting even less sleep than usual, frazzled from dealing with too many problems on both of her business ventures, and so ragged around the edges that it was showing in the lack of color in her face and the circles under her eyes, which she couldn't quite seem to conceal even when she had the time to try.

And on Friday morning she did make the time to try. That was the day Seth was due to clear out the Camden belongings from the attic and the barn.

She hadn't seen him at all since he'd left her at the guesthouse door on Monday night. She just hadn't spent enough time at home for it to happen. She regretted not seeing him, not getting to be with him. She'd still managed to be thinking about him more than she should have been, and daydreaming about him, and longing to hear his voice right in the midst of some of her worst crises at work.

So Friday—knowing that he was coming to the site—she sacrificed yet another half hour of sleep to get up early enough to make sure she could actually condition her hair, shape her eyebrows and work on covering up those dark circles before she added some color to her face with blush and applied mascara.

She also chose her clothing more carefully, opting for tan slacks that did a come-hither hug of her rear end, and a T-shirt adorned with a cluster of knit roses that cascaded from one shoulder diagonally across the front.

Then, rather than the simple ponytail that had been her quick and easy staple, she twisted her hair up the back of her head and left a geyser of curls at her crown so it was still out of her way but looked a little more done than the ponytail.

Unfortunately, Lacey was under fire when Seth arrived at the site Friday afternoon. She was in the middle of a phone call with her father, who was shouting at her. He claimed that if a man were in charge of the training center project, none of the disasters this week would have happened.

"Well, of course a man wouldn't have let any of it happen, Dad, because everyone knows that men have the ability to foresee the future and superpowers to keep the worst from happening!" Lacey retorted.

"Don't get smart with me, little girl. I saw you with Seth Camden at the wedding. He never left your side and you didn't seem to mind it too much. And you're living at his place—these things at the construction office better not be happening because you're paying more attention to him than to this job!"

"I'm staying in the guesthouse on the Camden ranch and I haven't even seen Seth since Monday night. I've been right here at the site for so many hours this week that I might as well have pitched a tent for myself. And nothing—*nothing*—that happened this week had *anything* to do with Seth Camden or could have been prevented or handled any differently by anyone else!" she insisted forcefully.

"Just make sure the training center is coming first."

It wasn't the first thing on her mind at that moment, when Lacey was all too aware that Seth was out at the barn and that she was hating that she wasn't out there with him. But still she said, "The training center *is* coming first. We just had a bad run after the groundbreaking but everything will be fine from here on."

Her father grumbled and groused some more before he finally let her off the phone. But that still didn't free Lacey to say hello to Seth, because as soon as she hung up with her father, the foreman came in to tell her that even when the crane arrived they wouldn't have an operator for it because the man they'd hired wasn't taking the job after all. And now Lacey needed to find them another one.

She was still in the middle of the new crisis when Seth left the barn and came into his family's former house to deal with the attic. All Lacey could do was wave to him when he poked his head into the dining room she used as her office, whisper for him to go ahead and do what he needed to do, and continue with the phone call she was in the middle of then.

At least as best she could when she kept losing her train of thought watching the big cowboy lug something out to his truck.

From her vantage point she couldn't see him until he got whatever he was taking out onto the front porch. But then, framed by the living room's picture window that she could see through from her desk because there was an open archway joining the dining room with the living room, she feasted on the sight of massively muscled arms beneath the short sleeves of his white T-shirt, thick thighs testing the denim of his jeans, broad shoulders flexed to their limit toting boxes stacked on top of boxes.

But just when she thought she might be able to get off the phone knowing that she had a new crane operator lined up, she saw Seth put what was apparently the last of his family's old belongings in the truck and raise the tailgate to lock it into place. Then he glanced back at the house, and when he saw through the window that she had her phone to her ear, he merely waved to signal that he was done and ready to leave.

And the only thing Lacey had been looking forward to all week—seeing Seth, getting to talk to him—wasn't going to happen.

"I'm sorry, I'm going to have to call you back," she said, cutting the call short so she could rush out the old house's front door to catch Seth.

"Hi!"

Okay, bursting out the door and saying that as breathlessly as she had was not how she'd planned to handle the situation. But it did stop Seth from getting behind the wheel and driving away without a word to her.

"Hey, stranger," he said with a forlorn sort of frown creasing his brow. He paused on the other side of the truck bed, leaning both of his arms on it and glancing at her. "Looked like you were busy—I didn't want to bother you…"

"'Busy' doesn't even cover it—I've been swamped all week."

He nodded, as if she wasn't telling him anything he hadn't already guessed. "Everything going okay?"

"No. It's been one disaster after another around here *and* with my sportswear business."

"Sorry to hear that," Seth said. But there seemed to be something removed and distant about him.

Lacey went down the porch steps and joined him on the other side of his truck bed, closing at least some of the physical distance between them. "Did you get everything?" she asked with a nod at the contents of his truck.

"I had one of my ranch hands follow me over in the truck with the trailer on it—he came in the back way. We got the rotary hoe—the farm equipment thingy, as you call it—loaded onto the trailer and Ross took it out of here after he helped me with the desk. He left a little while ago while I did the rest. But now I think you're free and clear—the place is all yours to do with as you please."

"Thanks."

Silence.

Lacey wondered why this seemed a little strained. A little awkward. Was it just because so much time had passed since they'd last seen each other?

Searching for something else to talk about in order to have a few more minutes of looking at that sharply drawn, sun-gilded face, she said, "What about that old trunk you found in the tackroom last week—did you have a key for the lock?"

"No key. I pried the lock off."

"What was inside?"

He gave a negligent shrug. "Nothing big. Some old journals. I barely looked at them. Sent them to my grandmother in Denver. You haven't run into anything else like that hidden away, have you?"

"No, I don't think so. Besides the groundbreaking, about the only work that got done around here this week was on the main part of the barn, getting it ready to store construction materials. I'm sure you saw that. But as far as I know no one found anything else that belonged to your family—"

"And you'd know if they did?"

Was this more important to him than he wanted to let on?

"I trust my crew, so yes, I'm sure if anyone found anything they would let me know."

"And then you'd let *me* know, right?"

"Well, sure. Are you missing something?"

"No," he was quick to say. "But we didn't know we'd left behind *this* stuff, either."

"If we come across anything more, I'll bring it to you

or tell you. You don't have to worry about me playing finders keepers."

He didn't smile at her joke. He was being very serious today...

"I'd appreciate it. For my grandmother's sake, you know."

"Sure," Lacey said.

Seth changed the subject then. "You weren't kidding when you asked to use the guesthouse and said I wouldn't even know you were around, were you? I haven't seen you all week."

"Tell that to my father. He seems to think I'm more interested in you than in the training center."

Oh, she wished she wouldn't have said that! Even if it did finally make Seth smile.

"I'm running neck and neck with the training center when it comes to your interests?" he asked.

She definitely wished she hadn't said that. It might have been true, but she didn't want him to know it.

"It's something stupid that my father accused me of because he saw us together at the wedding."

"Ahh..." The smile disappeared.

Just then, one of her crew bosses came around the side of the house from the barn and called to her in an ominous tone, saying that he thought she better take a look at their brick delivery.

"I'll let you get to work," Seth said, pushing off of the side of his truck without delay and opening the driver's door.

"Maybe I'll see you later," she said, not meaning for it to sound as hopeful as it did. But she was unhappy with how this brief encounter had gone, and she wanted some indication that it was all in her imagination.

Seth gave a shrug of one of those big shoulders as if it didn't matter to him one way or another—which was not at all reassuring. "You know where I live," he said offhandedly.

That didn't sound good, either.

But the crew boss called to her again, insisting that he wasn't kidding, that she'd better take a look at their brick order.

And Lacey had no choice but to move on to her latest problem before Seth had even started his engine.

It was nine o'clock that night before Lacey finished work and went back to the Camden guesthouse. There were no lights on in the main house when she arrived home—and it was Friday night and not too late—so she assumed that Seth was out for the evening.

And yes, again she was wondering if he might be with a woman, on a date. He'd said he didn't date much, but that didn't necessarily mean he didn't date at all...

Lacey hated the thought.

She told herself it was none of her business and that she had no reason to feel one way or another about it.

But still, demoralized and down in the dumps, she took a long shower and tried to wash away the week.

Then she did an at-home facial, put a deep conditioning mask on her hair, and sat for a while with pads over her eyes, hoping these measures would make her look rested.

It was ten-thirty before she concluded her self-pampering, and even though she was exhausted it still seemed too early to go to bed.

And no, she told herself, it wasn't because the main house remained dark and she was inclined to staying up to see when Seth got home and if he was alone when he did.

She just didn't want to go to bed yet.

So she blew her hair dry, left it loose around her shoulders, put on a pair of silky white pajama pants and a bright red crewneck, cap-sleeved T-shirt.

After that, realizing that she hadn't had anything to eat since lunch, she took a box of crackers out of the cupboard and dumped a pile of them onto a plate. Then she sliced a brick of cheese and took her handiwork outside to sit at the poolside table nearest to the guesthouse.

Not to wait for Seth. Just for the fresh air.

She didn't have long to not-wait, though, because by the time she was on her second cracker she heard his sports car come around from the front of the house to the garage.

Please don't let him have a date, she beseeched the fates, fully aware that it wasn't anything she should be asking of any higher power. That it was something she had no right to request. That it was something that shouldn't matter to her.

But she listened intently to the sound of his engine turning off, the car door opening and closing, and then the garage door closing, as well.

What she didn't hear was a second car door or voices that would lead her to believe he wasn't alone.

And her hopes rose like tiny helium-filled balloons freed of their moorings. Even though she was fully aware that their last meeting hadn't gone well and that she had no right to expect him to do anything more than say hello as he went into his house.

Then he came into the backyard and approached the

pool. He was by himself, dressed in khaki slacks and a yellow sport shirt, carrying a bottle of wine.

He caught sight of Lacey then and raised his chin at her, not smiling, merely acknowledging her.

"Hi," she said, forcing cheeriness.

"You're home. I'm amazed," he responded.

Lacey ignored that. "Night out?" she asked, trying to sound neutral.

"Dinner with friends."

"Didn't they like your wine selection?" she asked with a nod at the bottle he was carrying.

"They gave the wine to me. It was a thank-you for helping them move a couple of weeks ago."

"A *Camden* helped somebody move?" Lacey exclaimed as if it were unheard of, her anxieties over how he'd spent his evening and with whom lessening.

Seth did crack just a hint of a one-sided smile at that. "Believe it or not—last name notwithstanding—I can lift the end of a couch as well as the next guy. And it earned me a bottle of wine."

He seemed to hesitate a moment and Lacey was worried that a simple good-night was about to happen.

That was when—before she'd even thought about it—she heard herself say, "I have cheese and crackers. You have wine. We could combine our resources..."

"We could," he repeated noncommittally.

Lacey wasn't sure why it wasn't a simple yes or no. But it took him a moment before he seemed to concede and said, "Okay. I'll go in and open the wine and get glasses."

It would have been nice to see more enthusiasm, but still Lacey's energy level was instantly renewed, and the effects of her miserable week suddenly diminished as she watched Seth go to the house. After a few minutes, he returned to join her and pour the wine.

"You look unusually relaxed," he observed, as he handed her a glass and sat in the chair across from her.

Lacey slid the plate of cheese and crackers to the center of the small table. "I had a little winding-down time. It *didn't* involve a horse, but it was good anyway."

"You probably needed it. A couple of nights this week I wasn't sure if you made it home at all. You weren't here when I went to bed around midnight and you were gone again when I got up."

"There was just one night that I didn't make it home—I slept with my head on my desk. Luckily there's still a shower that works in the old house, and I keep a change of clothes in my car just in case."

"Just one night," he repeated. "And you keep a change of clothes in your car in case you don't get home from work because it happens often enough for you to need to be prepared?"

Lacey shrugged.

"But you honestly think that it's worth it—keeping this pace?" Seth asked, as if it were a concept he couldn't grasp.

"Wanting my work on the training center to make my father's jaw drop—plus keeping up with my clothing line—has made the pace worse than it ordinarily is. But I've always worked long hours and gone the extra mile. I'm not sure I'd know what to do with myself at any other pace," she admitted after a taste of the mildly fruity-tasting wine.

Seth took a drink. "That's good," he judged. "Good wine. Tonight I was with good friends, had good company and a good meal—"

"Things you don't think I take time for." Lacey guessed that that where he was heading with this.

"Things you *said* you don't take time for," he retorted. "Instead you drive around with a change of clothes in case you can't even get home to sleep."

"This project is important—I told you that, too."

He nodded but his expression showed pity. "No project, no *job,* should be *that* important. You need a life, too."

Feeling defensive, Lacey decided to turn the tables on him. "Okay, maybe you have more of a *life* than I do. And more friends—"

"More fun."

"But here you are, in the middle of nowhere—you *live* in a place we chose specifically because there won't be a lot of distractions for the team while they're training. You're out in the country, isolated. None of your family is here. You have friends who invite you to dinner, but what else? There's nothing much to do *but* work around here. I mean, I'm facing a weekend when nothing is going to happen at the construction site, with only some paperwork to catch up on, and I have to tell you, I'm dreading that I *won't* have my *pace* to keep me as busy as usual, because I'm not sure what I'm going to do around here."

Something about that made him smile genuinely—albeit a bit mischievously.

"You have the weekend off?" he asked, intrigued.

"After this weekend I'll have part of the crew working on Saturdays, but this past week was bad and nothing really got started, so there's nothing that can be done tomorrow. Like I said, I have paperwork to do—for the training center and for my sportswear collection—but other than that—"

"Give it to me, then," he challenged.

Lacey laughed. "Give *what* to you?"

"This weekend. Give me this weekend to show you how nice things can be around here when you *aren't* doing what you do. To show you how nice it can be when you aren't running around like crazy, when you just take some time to relax, to enjoy yourself. When you don't have to think about proving that you can do the work of three men. Or prove anything, for that matter. Tell your father you're spending the weekend at a convent or camping or something where he can't reach you—"

"My father is at a sports conference this weekend where he's the keynote speaker and will be wined and dined and the center of attention—I won't hear from him until it's over on Monday."

"Great! Then just be Lacey this weekend—not Lacey the overachiever, not Lacey the underdog-because-she's-a-girl, not Lacey who-needs-to-show-her-old-man-she-can-be-the-third-son-he-never-had, not Lacey the wonder-businesswoman. Just Lacey."

"Who's she?" Lacey joked.

"I'm not sure, but I think she might be somewhere between the pretty little princess her father got for her mother to play with, and one of the boys. But I'd kind of like to find out…"

He said that last part more quietly, as if he were admitting something he didn't want to admit.

But rather than think too much about what was going on with him, Lacey considered what he was suggesting. She really was worn-out. Two days of rest and relaxation might recharge her and make her that much more able to hit the next week head-on.

Except that it *was* two days with Seth.

Whom she shouldn't be spending concentrated periods of time with because she knew she was overly vulnerable to his looks, to his charm, to him.

But whom she really *wanted* to spend two days with.

"It's not as if I have the *whole* weekend free—I do have paperwork," she said.

"Hedging already!" he accused. "Then how about if I give you tomorrow morning to work? I have animals to feed and water, crops to check on. But after that, you've already said you don't know what you're going to do with yourself, remember?"

It *was* only two days and then she'd be back to business on all fronts, full throttle, she told herself.

"Can we talk about the new road I need?" she said.

Seth rolled his eyes. "No! You get tomorrow morning and that's it—the minute we're together there's no more work, no talk about work! Do you honestly not have any concept of what it is to take time off, to relax?"

"I need a road," she said.

"Okay, I'll make you a deal—this weekend in exchange for your damn road."

"Seriously?" she said hopefully.

"We will seriously come to terms on your road next week if you give me the next two days."

"Excluding mornings," she reminded.

"Excluding *tomorrow* morning," he qualified.

"Okay," Lacey said.

He offered a second glass of wine, but Lacey shook her head. "It's getting late," she pointed out, feeling fatigue creeping back in. "And I do have a lot of paperwork, so I'll have to get up early to make sure I can clear the afternoon."

"Whatever it takes," Seth said, putting the cork back in the bottle and getting up from the table when Lacey did.

But Lacey really was exhausted. As she stood she reached for the plate that held what remained of the cheese and crackers, but knocked it over, sending it crashing to the brick pavers that tiled the area surrounding the pool. The plate broke and the cheese and crackers went everywhere.

"And now you know that I get klutzy when I'm tired," she said.

"Better let me handle the broken glass, then." He came around the table to pick that up while Lacey retrieved the slices of cheese and the crackers. And stole a glance at Seth as he hunkered down on his heels, his thighs testing the fabric of his slacks.

Once they had the majority of the mess gathered up, they took the debris into the guesthouse to discard it. Then Lacey trailed Seth back to the door where they both stood straddling the threshold, spines against the opposite sides of the jamb so they could face each other.

"Will this weekend's portion of my lesson in relaxation involve hairy beasts?" Lacey asked at that point.

"Just me," he answered with a laugh.

He was hardly a hairy beast. Though his hair was really nice in its finger-combed, disheveled sort of way. And when it came to beastly he was anything but—that handsome face of his was all chiseled and gorgeous...

Lacey made herself concentrate on what he was saying.

"This is the weekend we celebrate Northbridge's

Founder's Day. There's a parade and all kinds of things going on tomorrow. Sunday there's the Founder's Day picnic out at the old bridge that the town is named for. It'll give you a taste of what goes on around here and how nice it is to just be a part of it."

"And if I get bored out of my mind?" she joked.

"Oh, I'm not gonna let *that* happen," he answered with a touch of the devil in his voice.

Lacey laughed, but she realized that somehow in that instant the tone had changed between them altogether. That they'd gone from Seth being distant and her being desperate for him not to be, to sharing friendly banter and teasing and exchanging a few challenges, to the chemistry that was always just beneath the surface.

Now, standing in that doorway, Seth was looking down at her, his eyes, slightly hooded and mesmerizing, searching hers....

"What is there about you," he muttered, shaking his head.

What was there about *him?*

What was there that made her so sensitive to everything to do with him, so sensitive when something was off between them that nothing felt right until she was with him and things were okay again?

What was there about him that made everything else fade into insignificance, that lifted her spirits and restored her spent energies, that left her wanting nothing so much as him?

He brought a hand around to the back of her neck and up into her hair, and Lacey gave over control just that easily. She let him tilt her head as he leaned forward, not resisting at all when his mouth found hers, answering the parting of his lips by parting hers, too.

And why, in that instant, did she feel as if all really was right with the world again?

Her eyes closed and her head fell back into his big hand as she placed a palm lightly on his chest—feeling the hardness of muscle behind his shirt and absorbing the power and strength hidden there.

He urged her lips to part more still and when they did, he sent his tongue to tease hers.

Glittery sensations rained all through her at that bit of increased intimacy, at that kiss that deepened and went where she'd longed for their kiss in the barn to go.

Lacey's awareness of everything else fell away and it was the man alone, the kiss alone, that carried her beyond her own weariness, that infused her and lifted her at once and made her melt.

But just as other hungers began to awaken in her, Seth brought the kiss to a slow conclusion, retreating, then roguishly returning only to retreat again before the kiss grew more sensual than sexy, then chaste and sweet, then ended altogether.

When it did, Lacey opened her eyes. His face was still very close to hers.

"Tomorrow. Noon. Then no more work," he said in a deep voice.

"Yeah, yeah, yeah, I remember," she said sassily, making him smile.

He let go of her, dipping his chin to kiss the top of her head, and then moved out of the doorway.

"Leave the rest of this mess out here, I'll sweep and hose it off tomorrow," he ordered, as he walked around the remnants of glass and crackers.

Lacey had forgotten all about that. She nodded and shut the door, letting her eyes drift closed again so she could go on savoring the lingering sensation, the lingering memory of that kiss for another moment.

Before she reminded herself that things like that shouldn't be going on between them.

And then went to bed longing for more anyway...

Chapter Eight

"Hey, I just swung by the training center site hoping to catch you, and you weren't there."

"No, I'm not there," Lacey confirmed, feeling a sudden rush of panic. It was 10:00 a.m. on Saturday morning when her cell phone rang and she answered the call from her brother Ian. "Did Dad send you out to check on me?"

"No, no, nothing like that."

"I'm doing paperwork at home," she added. "It was a bad week—Dad knows that—and it wasn't cost-effective to have the crew come in this weekend when they couldn't accomplish anything substantial, so I'm catching up on—"

"Paperwork," her brother finished for her. "Honest, Lace, I'm not spying for Dad."

She had to work twice as hard, be twice as diligent and worry twice as much that anyone would think she was slacking off—it came with the territory of proving to her father that she could do the work of a man, and Lacey was accustomed to it. But maybe she didn't have to be so worried when it came to her brother.

On the other hand, the training center project had been Ian's, and he might be hoping she would fail so he could take over again...

Lacey hated herself for that thought. Ian had never done anything to her that was backstabbing or cutthroat, and he didn't deserve that.

"I haven't seen or heard from you since the wedding, so I just wanted to check in," Ian explained. "Jenna and Abby and I are leaving town this afternoon—Jenna has a friend in Billings we're seeing this weekend—and I just thought I'd let you know, and make sure you didn't need anything before I go."

"You'll be gone this whole weekend?" Lacey asked, trying to keep her tone neutral. But it wasn't easy. With Ian gone, Hutch still on his honeymoon, and no chance that her father would show up, the sudden feeling of freedom was heady.

"The whole weekend, yeah," Ian confirmed. "We won't be back until Monday."

Lacey couldn't help but smile. "Thanks, but no, I don't need anything," she said, trying to keep from giving away her feelings.

"So how is everything going with you?" her brother asked. "Are you doing all right living at the Camden place?"

"It's just somewhere to drop when I finally leave work at night."

"Sure," Ian said as if he would expect nothing less.

"Did you know that Seth Camden told Dad that he wasn't a fan of football?"

Lacey wondered if Ian had suspicions that something was going on between her and Seth and was giving her fair warning. "Yes. I heard them at the wedding."

"Is it true?"

"I guess," Lacey answered.

"Even if he is a Camden, you know what that means to Dad—"

"If you're not a football fan, you're nothing." Her father had said it more times than she could count.

"I like Seth, though," Ian offered as if in consolation, making her think he definitely had suspicions about what was going on between them. "I've talked to him a dozen or so times since I've been here—at one function or another, or just meeting him on the street—and he seems like a good guy."

"He is," Lacey confirmed.

"Are you seeing much of him?"

She hoped this was about her brother's own curiosity and that he wasn't on a fishing expedition their father had sent him on.

"Our paths rarely cross," she said. Then, not wanting to talk about Seth, she changed the subject. "When are Hutch and Issa and Ash due back from their honeymoon?"

"Monday, I think. I hear your clothes are doing big things in his stores—are you trying to keep up with that on top of the training center?"

"I am," she said.

"Wow, you've got your hands full."

"I do. Plus I had three people working my supply and distribution center, and my shippers quit. The two people left are going crazy, and I've had to let them try to find a replacement because I just can't get to Billings to do it myself."

"I should probably let you get back to work then." Lacey didn't argue. "Have a good trip."

"We will. I'll see you when we get back."

"Okay." They said goodbye and hung up.

Almost instantly her thoughts turned to Ian's comment about Seth not being a football fan.

Had her brother been making a point of it?

Seth had admitted that he could take football or leave it. Trying to fit that into the super-jock-live-and-breathe-football-club that was the Kincaids? Not likely.

It was just something that she kept telling herself she had to keep in mind when it came to resisting any attraction to Seth.

Intelligent, strong, interesting, funny, staggeringly handsome and sexy as he could possibly be—that all might be true of the man, but none of it could carry more weight than the things that she knew dictated that they stay apart.

Camden or not, he was all easygoing country boy and she was anything but a nature-loving girl, even if she had been born and raised in Montana.

And while Seth might be great to relax with, to wind down with, that laid-back thing he did so well was not Lacey. A slower pace would likely drive her crazy in the long run because she liked to be going and doing and working and as busy as she could keep herself.

Put it all together and it added up to her and Seth being two people who couldn't be more wrong for each other.

And you'd better remember that! she told herself.

She'd better remember it all through today and tomorrow when she was with him, and not give in too much to that attraction.

Doing the Founder's Day festival with him was just a way to fill some time she had on her hands. She wouldn't let it become any more than that.

She wouldn't.

But could she pull that off?

That tiny whisper of doubt floated around the back of her mind.

No, she wasn't one hundred percent sure she could.

In fact, she wasn't even one percent sure.

Saturday afternoon brought the Founder's Day parade. Many Northbridge natives dressed in historic costume, representing their ancestors by walking the parade route or, in some cases, riding in old buggies, horse-drawn wagons or carriages.

There were marching bands and placards with pictures of the town in its earliest incarnations, along with pictures of the original founders and other people thought to have brought expansion and progress to Northbridge. It was on one of those that an old photograph of H. J. Camden was displayed. As it went by, there were several *boo*s called from various spots in the crowd.

Uncomfortable with that, Lacey glanced up at Seth, who was standing by her side. He showed no indications of having heard the jeers and merely went on watching the parade.

When it ended they walked through the maze of booths in the Town Square to the gazebo. There they watched Miss Northbridge be crowned, sat through the dance performance of a troop of local eight-year-old girls and several songs sung by the local church choir and then the barbershop quartet. Then they listened to the speeches given by the mayor and two of the city councilmen.

Dinner was a potluck held under an enormous white tent, and Seth and Lacey ended up eating with a group of Seth's friends.

After that they strolled in the direction of the college campus, touring the display where the placards with the pictures of early Northbridge, its founders and its most important citizens had been put up.

Someone had hung a black shroudlike scarf over the portrait of Seth's great-grandfather.

Lacey took a sideways glance at Seth, who calmly strode up to the picture, removed the scarf to put in a nearby trash receptacle and stepped back to Lacey's side.

Before she'd thought of what to say about that, Seth said, "There's always two camps—the ones who think old H.J. brought progress and good, and the ones who say he made his way on the backs of other people."

"Even around here? In his hometown?" Lacey asked cautiously.

"Oh, sure. This is where H.J. started out. He was a scrappy guy, determined to make something of himself. The property you're turning into your training facility was originally a farm and a lumber mill operated in the barn—H.J.'s folks owned it."

"H.J.'s roots."

"Right. From the minute H.J. was old enough to work, he did, saving every penny until he could start buying up timberland outside of Northbridge. The timberland contained a gold mine that was thought to be played out—"

"That's right. I remember something from my class about him actually striking gold."

"Not a whole lot of it, but yeah, he managed to find a vein that gave him the money to make his next and most important purchase—a chunk of land that was rich in iron deposits. Of course it's been said that he knew that was the case before he bought the land for next to nothing and duped the previous owners who *didn't* know about the iron deposits. It's also been said that by reopening the gold mine and mining the iron, he put people to work and kept Northbridge going when farming wasn't paying—like I told you, two camps."

"Then he left Northbridge?"

"In his twenties, after he had enough of a bankroll. But he kept what he owned here, and when he wanted to use Northbridge as a retreat he came back, bought even more land. But he was always looking for the best deal, so he bought from people who were struggling and about to lose their farms, so there are those who say he capitalized on the misfortunes of others to build what we own now."

"If people needed to sell their property and he bought it, that's just business," Lacey said.

Seth smiled tentatively. "Sure. But then there are also the contentions that he manipulated things in his favor, that he had powerful people in his pocket, so water rights were redistributed, or property lines redrawn to his advantage."

"Is that true?"

He shrugged. "I couldn't tell you. My great-grandfather, my grandfather, my father and my uncle—

they all kept the business far, far away from us when we were kids. I do know that my father and my uncle started the policy of giving back—of getting involved in charities and organizations that benefited other people. The negative side says that was just to clean up the Camden name and reputation, to put a better face on wrongdoings. I can tell you that from my standpoint—and my brothers' and sister's and cousins' standpoint—we're all vigilant about anything to do with Camden Incorporated being on the up-and-up now."

"I know that there can be sour grapes when it comes to success," Lacey said. "We run into it. Even during my dad's football career, there were players he beat out for starter position who claimed he didn't deserve it, that he played dirty or that he made it for some other reason. And of course in business it's been said that he's only gotten where he is on his name. To some extent, resentment is unavoidable and you just have to live with it."

"And hope it's unfounded," Seth said so quietly she wasn't sure she was meant to hear it. She thought better of responding.

Then, in a normal octave, he added, "But H.J. was always good to me and I loved the old coot, so here's to you, H.J." He tapped his temple with two fingers and gave the photograph a casual salute.

Then he turned to Lacey and said, "Now how about you and I go dancing?"

"So you *do* dance?" she said.

"Yep," he answered with a smile. "I can't promise that I'm the best you'll ever come across, but I know how. And it's Saturday night and I can hear the music starting up, and here we are—seems like we should…

Unless you don't like to dance…you weren't in favor of it at your brother's wedding."

"That was different. I love to dance, I just rarely get to. But I'm not dressed for it," she said. For dancing she would have worn something less confining than her butt-hugging jeans and more supportive than the white chiffon tank top with its cascading frilly front and built-in bra. And she wouldn't have worn sandals.

"It's the Founder's Day dance in the Square. We don't need to be dressed up." Seth glanced down at his own Western shirt with the long sleeves rolled to his elbows, the jeans that he looked too good to be true in and his cowboy boots. "I could probably do some damage to your bare toes, but I promise to be extra careful not to step on them, if you're game."

She was. Carried away by that sense of freedom, Lacey didn't hesitate a moment more. "Okay," she said.

He reached down and took her hand. Then he put it in the crook of his arm and kept his own hand over hers, tucking her securely into his side, where she instantly got to come up against that big body of his.

She'd been having a good time up to that point; suddenly having physical contact with Seth just made it all the better.

And the thought that she was about to dance with him left her almost giddy and feeling a little like someone who could throw everything else away just for the chance.

At least for tonight.

Lacey had to give Northbridge credit—the little town knew how to kick up its heels. The entire wooden dance floor at the steps of the gazebo was filled with couples,

couples carrying kids, teenagers and even a few preteen girls, all dancing to the music played by a local band positioned in the gazebo itself. And nearly everyone was dressed as casually as she and Seth were.

Friendly, relaxed and fun—that was purely and simply what it was, and Lacey gave herself over to it and to the pleasure of being with Seth.

They danced almost every dance. He never once stepped on her toes, and while the joy and merriment all around them contributed to Lacey's good time, it was Seth she focused on to such an extent that she didn't even notice when the crowd was thinning or the hour was growing late. So the announcement of the last dance came as a surprise to her.

And as sorry as she was to hear it, she was at least grateful that the last dance was a slow one. Seth swung her into his arms, pulling her close before he clasped his hands at the small of her back.

"You underestimated yourself," she told him, her own hands on his shoulders, wanting to lay her cheek on his chest but peering up at him instead. "You're a great dancer."

"Or maybe it was just my partner who made me look good," he countered. "You never missed a beat—I'm thinking you must have had lessons."

"Years of them. We all did. Mom insisted on them for Ian and Hutch because she wanted them doing something—*anything*—that wasn't football. She'd gotten me started about a year before she died, but my dad kept me going because he thought girls needed to know how to dance."

"Did he let your brothers quit?"

"No, by then he'd decided that it helped their agility

on the football field, so he kept them in the class, too. What about you?" she said. "Lessons?"

"In high school—there was an extracurricular class offered, and not only did my friends and I figure it would be an easy A, we also got the idea that it was a way to hook up with girls."

"Ahh," Lacey said with a laugh. "Was it?"

He grinned. "Oh yeah!"

Then he perched his chin on the top of her head and talking didn't seem necessary. Instead it was just nice to sway to the music. To be there with him. To have his arms around her. And Lacey merely went with the flow of it all, a little amazed by how well they seemed to fit together, to move together, to do everything together...

So yes, she was sorry to have that last song end. And their last dance with it. But for a moment longer Seth went on swaying, not letting her go, keeping his chin to her head.

Only when the other dancers finished clapping and whistling and thanking the band, and began to leave, did he take a deep breath that made his chest rise and fall very near to her face, sigh the breath out into her hair and release her.

But what softened the blow of that dance and the evening coming to an end was when he held her hand as they headed for his car.

"I had a really good time," she confided along the way. "Since high school I've hardly ever gotten to dance."

"You haven't dated dancers?" he joked.

"No. On the rare occasions when I've dated, danc-ing hasn't been on the menu."

"Rare occasions, huh?" he repeated with a sideways

glance at her. "Let me guess—you've done more working than dating."

"Yep," she said, mimicking the clipped answer he frequently gave.

"But there *was* a fiancé," he reminded.

"There was," she confirmed. She'd told him that on Monday night after the groundbreaking, when they were sitting by the pool. And she knew he listened intently to what she said and recalled it all, so it only followed that he'd retained that bit of information.

"How did you get engaged to somebody if you didn't date?" Seth asked once they were settled in the car.

"I dated a little. But nothing long-term or serious. Until Dominic."

"Tell me about him—or is that off-limits?"

It wasn't a subject she *liked* talking about. But she did like that Seth was up front with his curiosity and not using any kind of subterfuge to get answers out of her.

"No, it's not off-limits," she said, deciding in the moment that that was true. "Dominic Salvadi. He's a hotshot criminal defense attorney."

"I've heard of him. He's in the news. He seems to end up representing any high-profile case that comes up in Montana."

"Yes, he does."

"How did you meet him? Or did I miss that you were accused of committing a heinous crime that he defended you for?"

"I swear it wasn't me who murdered my last landlord, and I don't know who did," Lacey said theatrically.

Seth laughed as he drove out of Northbridge proper and headed for his ranch. "That's a relief to *this* landlord," he joked.

"I met Dominic at a party. We had a friend in common."

"Love at first sight?"

"No, we just sort of hit it off. He asked me out and it went from there, the way those things do—first it was a dinner, then there was a concert a week later."

Although she didn't remember caring as much about going a week without seeing Dominic as she'd cared this last week about not seeing Seth…

"Anyway," she continued, shooing that thought out of her mind, "we dated for a year, then moved in together. We lived together for two years and were engaged for the last six months of that time."

"But no marriage. What happened?"

Lacey shrugged, but they were driving through the dark countryside and she doubted that Seth had seen it. "I broke up with him."

"Just like that? Not a big deal— "

Is that how she'd made it sound?

"Breaking up *was* a big deal—we lived together, owned things together, had wedding plans, our future mapped out. It wasn't as easy as *I just don't want to see you again.*"

"But you seem nonchalant about it now."

"I didn't catch him in bed with someone or anything like that. I just…" Another shrug. "It was just *things*…"

"Things," Seth parroted, to prompt her to go on.

"Two things," Lacey said tentatively, unsure if her reasons ever seemed strong enough to other people when she shared them.

But after considering it a moment, she decided that it was not altogether bad to let Seth know what her reasons were.

"On the surface, the issue was that Dominic had absolutely no interest in football," she said then. "He hadn't seen a handful of games in his entire life, he was nearly football illiterate, and he couldn't have cared less about it."

"And that was a problem?"

"I didn't care so much about it—in fact, it was kind of a relief to get away from football sometimes. But my father *is* Kincaid Corporation, and he eats, sleeps, breathes, lives and dies for the game. I needed Dominic to show just a tiny bit of interest in it the way anyone would need the person they're with to show an interest in something their boss is obsessed with, the way you'd hope someone you're partnering with for life would do with your father."

"And this guy wouldn't?"

"Absolutely not. He would not be bothered. He wasn't interested in football and that was it. End of story. Even though football is *everything* my family is about."

"Are you saying that it was something you specifically asked him to do for you?"

"Because it was important to me both for my job and to be a part of my family."

"And he flat-out refused."

"Flat-out," Lacey confirmed. "Which made my life more difficult with a father who also happens to be my boss. It was just one more step outside of the boys' club for me."

"And essentially you felt like the guy you were with was doing damage to your career because he wouldn't give a little."

"And just a little was all I was asking so he and I wouldn't be relegated to the sidelines when it came to my father. But like I said, that was just the surface issue, and what I started to see was that there was an even bigger problem with Dominic—like the fact that the longer things went on, the more Dominic showed signs of being *like* my father."

"Signs of being like your father?" Seth echoed her words. "And you *didn't* appreciate that?"

Lacey laughed wryly. "You think that someone who reminds me of my father would be more appealing to me?"

Seth shrugged. "Sometimes that happens."

Lacey laughed at the notion. "I'm not neurotic about my father. I want to be a major player in the Kincaid Corporation. I deserve to be. I have a rightful place in the business I cut my teeth on, and I've been denied any *real* opportunity until now solely because I'm not a man. If anything, it's just that I'm competitive and I'm determined to prove myself and earn the rank that got handed to my brothers on a silver platter."

"Seems like competition was probably ingrained in you from the minute Morgan Kincaid became your father."

Lacey couldn't refute that.

"So the bigger issue with this Dominic guy was that he reminded you of your dad," Seth prompted. "How so?"

"Dominic started to talk about how he didn't want me to work after we got married. How he could *provide* for me and he wanted me at home, taking care of *his* houses, *his* kids. And when it came to my *little* clothing line, he let me know he saw that as my hobby, but he didn't think that should be kept up, either."

"You hate it when your father calls you *little girl*—

I saw you flinch. *Little* clothing line pushed that same button," Seth guessed, impressing her with his perception.

"It did. And Dominic's whole attitude, the whole male-superiority thing, just made me look at him and see my father, and it was a *huge* turnoff. There was no way I was getting into a marriage with someone who had the same view of women that my father has."

"You've already had to fight that for too long," Seth agreed as he pulled onto the road that led to his property.

"So that was it for me. I cared about him…" Her voice went quiet again. "I loved him, and it wasn't easy to call it off. But it's bad enough to have my father think what he's always thought of me. I didn't want to marry that same narrow-mindedness. I didn't want to fight it in a marriage, too, or have kids—potentially daughters— and raise them with a father like that."

"I think that was a really wise choice."

Lacey laughed as he drove around the main house and into the garage. "I don't know how wise I am. Stubborn—that's been said of me. But no one has ever called me wise before. At least not in a good way."

"But you've never killed a landlord, so how bad can you be?" he teased her, turning off the engine.

Getting out of the car laid that subject to a natural rest. They walked together to the guesthouse in a moment of silence.

Not until Lacey had unlocked and opened the door did Seth say, "Sooo…you made it. An entire afternoon and evening without working."

Again Lacey laughed. "And I didn't even miss it— maybe there *are* a few lazy bones in this body."

He glanced downward at the body in question and

smiled appreciatively. "I definitely don't think we can say anything negative about the body," he muttered.

Lacey didn't respond. Instead she repeated what she'd said when they'd left the dance. "I did have a really good time, though."

"And there's still a day to go."

She made a face. "Yeah. Any chance we could do tomorrow the way we did today and I could have the morning to do paperwork again? I didn't get it all finished this morning."

"I suppose. But only because I have animals to feed and water, a field to check on—"

"Oh, I get it—it's okay if you need to work," she goaded.

"Hey, hey, hey, don't go trying to make me into your old man or the lawyer. I'm not saying what I do is more important than what you do. I'm just saying that what you do, you do too much of. To the exclusion of everything else. There needs to be a balance."

He leaned a forearm high up on the door frame and switched his weight to one hip. The change of position brought him in closer to Lacey, who was standing in the threshold.

"I had a really good time, too," he admitted, his voice deeper, more intimate.

His bright cobalt-blue eyes peered so intensely into hers that the two of them, and that moment, were suddenly all there was. And after her taste of being in his arms in public, on the dance floor, Lacey nearly ached with wanting to be in his arms again now—without anyone else around.

It was that urge that brought her hand up to his cheek. He covered that hand with his own, curving his fingers around it, pulling it down to hold at his chest—his broad, hard chest—freeing himself to lean forward and capture her mouth with his.

Lacey closed her eyes and let herself drift off toward what seemed like heaven.

There was a familiarity between them now. A familiarity that left few reservations. Their lips parted without hesitation, freeing the way for his tongue to make an almost instant appearance, which Lacey welcomed.

She let her other hand rest on his chest, too, moving in nearer, tilting her head more and presenting a better angle for their kiss.

Seth wrapped his arm around her to bring her up against him as commandingly as when he'd led on the dance floor.

She slipped her hand out from under his in order to raise her arms up and over his shoulders, pressing her breasts against his chest—something she'd longed for all evening. Her nipples turned to steely little pebbles that craved even more.

She wondered if Seth could feel them. His shirt wasn't heavy, and her chiffon tank top wasn't much of a barrier, either—even with the built-in bra and even if it *did* seem to her like armor.

He might have been aware of what was going on with her because he moved in closer, holding her tighter and taking them both over the threshold and slightly into the guesthouse. His mouth opened even wider over hers, and his tongue began to play a sensuous game of cat and mouse.

He spun her around then—as if they were still dancing—and Lacey found herself with her back to the wall beside the door, trapped between it and Seth in the love-liest way.

One of his hands went up the side of her neck and into her hair, as both of hers did a survey of his expansive back—all the hills and valleys formed by muscles made of steel. She dug her fingers into them, wanting that shirt out of her way.

It came free of his jeans without much trouble, and that seemed like an invitation to her. So she slipped her hands underneath the shirt and savored her first contact with his warm, satiny skin.

Her hands glided over every inch of that back. She trailed her fingers along his spine. She fanned them out over his massive shoulders. She massaged the curve of his rib cage.

And he must have liked it, because their kiss turned hotter, sexier, more demanding with every stroke.

His hand began a descent from her hair, and hope erupted in Lacey.

Keep going... Keep going... Keep going...

He did, from her neck to her shoulder. From her shoulder to her upper arm. From her upper arm to the side of her waist.

Too far!

Her tongue gave his an impudent little jab that made him smile even as he gave as good as he got.

And then his hand rose up her side to the outer swell of her breast.

It was unintentional, but on their own her shoulders drew back and pushed her chest out, revealing what she wanted all too blatantly.

But still he took his time, continuing to kiss her into near oblivion, to hold her to him.

Then that hand at the very edge of her breast finally came around front, finally engulfed her and gave her nipple the curve of his palm to nestle into.

It felt so good. Too bad her tank top was in the way.

Lacey brought her own hands around to the front of his shirt, spending a moment enjoying the feel of his honed pectorals, of his taut male nipples, before she let her hands traipse down his flat belly.

Ooo, it was tempting to just keep going. Inside his waistband, behind his zipper...

But she stopped herself and instead finessed his shirttails from his jeans in front, then fanned her arms and in one outward motion unsnapped all the buttons of his shirt.

That elicited a rumbling sort of chuckle in his throat as Lacey's hands rose again to his chest and delivered the full hint that she wanted him to get past the barrier of her shirt, too.

A hint he wasted no time in acting on. He quickly slid his hand under her tank top, under the shelf of a bra, engulfing her very engorged flesh in the heat of his unfettered grasp.

The man could dance.

The man could kiss like no one she'd ever kissed before.

But oh, what he did with that hand!

There were wonders to be had at Seth's touch. Gentle and tender. Tougher, rougher just when she needed it to be. Teasing and toying and playful. He kneaded her breast, he massaged and rubbed, tickled and tugged, circled and subdued and altogether worked Lacey into a frenzy of desires that sprang to life throughout her body.

Her head was back against the wall, her mouth plundered by his even as she did some plundering of her own. Her spine was arched to press her breasts into his grasp. And as her body began to crave even more she kicked aside her sandal and let her bare foot climb slowly up his calf.

And before she knew it, she was partially straddling his thigh and on the verge of taking things further....

Which was oddly when—for no reason she understood—she remembered that this Founder's Day weekend was supposed to be just a way to fill some time, that she'd sworn to herself not to let it become more than that. With Seth. To keep in mind why she needed not to let it become more than a time-filler. With Seth.

And this—and where she wanted this to go from here—was more than a time-filler. Much, much more.

So much more that it suddenly sent a ripple of uneasiness through Lacey.

She could be risking everything to let this go any further...

"Okay, okay, okay—we have to stop," she said breathlessly after tearing away from their kiss.

"We do?" he asked in a raspy voice that enticed all by itself.

"We do," Lacey decreed before she could think twice about it. She knew that to hesitate was to give in to what her entire body, her entire being, was screaming for.

Still he gave it one more try, kissing her fervently but also sweetly and intriguingly at once, and giving her breast a deep, earnest press that made her wish that he'd never take his hand from there.

But that ripple of uneasiness continued to shimmy through her; she couldn't ignore it.

"No, I mean it, we really do have to stop..." she insisted when he ended their kiss a moment later.

One final, lingering press of her breast, and he slipped his hand out from under her shirt. Lacey couldn't help the moan of disappointment that went with it.

"You're sure?" he asked after he'd kissed her again, glancing down at her leg still wrapped around his, keeping him in place despite what she'd said.

Lacey gave a chagrined laugh. "Yeah," she said, taking her foot off his calf and nearly melting at the feel of his hand on the back of her thigh when he clasped it to help ease her leg down.

Another kiss—such a good, good kiss—and he backed away, putting distance she regretted between them.

"Guess I'll see you tomorrow, then."

Lacey could only manage to nod. He sidestepped to the open door of the guesthouse and went out.

She took a deep breath and told herself she'd done the right thing.

But she also turned so she could watch Seth walk around the pool.

He hadn't snapped the buttons on his shirt closed, or tucked in the tails she'd pulled free, and watching those shirttails flap around his hips, knowing that the front of his shirt was open, exposing that chest she'd felt but hadn't actually seen, only made her want to call to him. To get him to turn around so she could see it.

But before she'd done that he reached the main house and let himself in through the French doors.

Then she got her wish when he turned around to close the door. Through the glass she saw just a strip of that chest, of his flat belly and the treasure trail of dark hair that went from his navel to disappear behind the zipper of his low-slung jeans...

Oh, but the man was gorgeous, and Lacey nearly came away from leaning against that wall. She nearly shot out her own door to join him across the way, to leap into his arms, to put herself against that chest again and allow her body what it craved so much she was in a private little misery all her own.

But in the end, reason prevailed. She knew she had too much at stake, so she merely groaned, reached across the open doorway and put the door in a death grip to close it.

Then she shut her eyes and wondered if anything was worth feeling the unquenched desires and longings that were all she was left with...

Chapter Nine

"Another early phone call, and this one on a Sunday—that doesn't speak well of your Saturday night or your social life," Seth goaded his brother Cade, who called at seven-thirty the next morning.

"Yeah, well, I don't hear a female voice in the background there, either, so my money is on you spending last night alone, too," Cade countered.

Alone and in near agony, Seth wanted Lacey so bad he'd been up half the night pacing and looking out at the guesthouse, willing her to change her mind and come to him.

Then he'd told himself all the reasons why she'd been right not to let things go any further than they had.

Seth decided to one-up his brother. "I *was* out with a woman last night. This is Northbridge's Founder's Day weekend, and I took Lacey Kincaid to yesterday's events. We danced until after midnight." *And then came home to do more than dance…*

But he didn't say that. There was something about Lacey, about what was happening between them, that he didn't want to cheapen. That he wanted to keep private and *just* between the two of them.

Apparently Cade had more on his mind, though, because he let the brotherly bantering end there and said, "I had dinner with GiGi last night—she hasn't been herself since she got those journals you sent, and I thought it might do her some good to get out."

"Is something wrong with GiGi?" Seth asked, suddenly concerned for their grandmother's health.

"The journals are what's wrong with GiGi."

"Should I not have sent them?"

"No, it's not that. In fact she told me something last night that she hasn't told any of us, something that she said she's tried to forget about since H.J. died, but now the journals confirm it."

"What did she tell you?"

"Apparently during those last weeks with H.J.— when he was in and out of it, sometimes making sense and sometimes not—he told her about some things he'd done. Business things. How he'd wheeled and dealed to make things go his way. He talked about paying off politicians, tampering with a jury, driving people off land he wanted—"

"The worst of what's been said of him and of Gramps."

"GiGi said he also kept saying something about a record of things or maybe a record book—"

"So he told her about the journals?"

"That isn't what he called them, and she thought

he was talking more about there being a record of his life—like a religious kind of thing that might affect his afterlife or something. You know how H.J. was at the end—he was rambling and confused, he was seeing things and people who weren't there, talking crazy a lot of the time and not making sense. GiGi said she didn't pay any attention to the record-book talk, and she just hoped the more serious things he was saying weren't true."

"But they were," Seth said direly.

"She's only just scratched the surface of the journals, but she showed me a couple of things in what she's read so far," Cade said. Then, as if he were admitting something he didn't want to admit, he added, "It isn't good, Seth. In fact, it might be worse than what everyone's always said about us."

Seth didn't want to believe that. "You're kidding."

"I wish I was. But apparently the old man—and Gramps, too—didn't let anything or anyone get in their way."

"And Dad and Uncle Mitchum?"

"I don't know yet. But what I do know is that just from the little I read last night, if anything in those journals ever got out, donations and charity work and funding wings in hospitals and buildings for colleges and the fact that our practices now are strictly on the straight and narrow wouldn't be enough."

"Geez…"

"Yeah. The guys we knew our great-grandfather and grandfather to be, might really—*really*—not have been the same guys they were when it came to building Camden Incorporated."

"So we can't let anything in those journals get out," Seth said, going back to his brother's earlier comment.

"No, we can't," Cade agreed. "But I'm not sure GiGi is going to let it go, either."

"What does that mean?"

"She's rocked by this. She said she never paid much attention to the negative things that were said about us, that she chose to believe that what H.J. was confiding in her at the end wasn't true. But now the blinders are off and some things might need to be made right."

"What *things?*" Seth asked, new concerns rising in him.

"She wouldn't say. She said she's going to make sure she's read through everything by her birthday and we'll talk about it then."

"How shook up is she?" Seth said. "This isn't going to cause *her* to stroke out or something, is it? I mean, I know she seems to be in good health, but she *is* going to be seventy-five and we can't let old sins that weren't even hers take a toll on her."

"I tried to get her to give me the journals, to stop reading them. I told her I'd go through them and just give her the Cliff Notes. But she wouldn't even consider it. You know GiGi—"

"Stubborn and probably thinking to protect us. So she'll read the journals, try to filter out the worst and only give us the Cliff Notes."

Cade laughed. "Right. But beyond her being quiet and preoccupied—and showing the kind of determination she showed when she took us all in after the plane crash—I didn't see any signs that this was taking a toll on her health. Her cheeks were still rosy, she spotted a loose button on my jacket that she had to sew and she'd baked me cookies to take home with me—"

"Chocolate chip or oatmeal raisin?"

"Oatmeal raisin."

"Damn you! I haven't had GiGi's oatmeal raisin cookies in a year!"

"That's what you get for living in Montana," Cade said in a gloating tone. "Anyway, I think she's okay, but I'll keep an eye on her. I just thought I'd let you know that we dodged a bullet by finding those journals ourselves, and if anyone else knows we did—"

"Lacey asked if there was anything in the trunk and I told her the truth. But I didn't make the journals sound interesting at all. She's probably forgotten by now. And no one but me saw them."

"Lacey Kincaid again. Huh…"

"She's was with me when I found the trunk," Seth explained, a little annoyed by his brother's suspicious tone.

"Well, from here on we'd better keep it plenty quiet that those journals exist," Cade said. "Even when it comes to Lacey Kincaid."

"No problem," Seth assured.

And that was the truth. When he was with Lacey the last thing on his mind was an old trunk, the journals that were inside of it, or what those journals might reveal about the sins of his forefathers.

"And be warned," Cade said. "When you come for GiGi's birthday we'll probably have to deal with this."

"Sure. In the meantime, don't let GiGi get upset over any of it. Make sure she knows that we'll take care of it."

"I'm doing the best I can, but she's all up in arms already. Last night she said H.J. and Gramps should be glad they're dead, because if they weren't she might kill them herself. Something in the journals hit her too close to home. She said there was one thing that was personal, and she doesn't know how she's going to live with it now that she knows about it."

"What could that be?"

"Your guess is as good as mine. She wouldn't elaborate. She pursed her lips together that way she does when she's so mad she's afraid of what she might say, and I know better than to push her when she does that."

"Her birthday ought to be interesting, then—is that what you're telling me?"

"I'd bet on it."

After working all of Sunday morning in raggedy shorts and a tank top for the Founder's Day picnic, Lacey showered and shampooed her hair, and changed into a lightweight, mid-calf-length black halter dress with a bright paisley print.

She wasn't sure about wearing the dress. Not only did it leave her arms and shoulders bare, it had an Empire waist with a neckline that dipped to within two inches of the band that ran just below her breasts. She wondered if it might be a little risqué for a small-town family picnic.

But she loved the dress. It kept her cool, the skirt was flowy and it made her feel feminine and about as far from work and business suits or construction-site jeans as she could get. And since the goal of the weekend was to escape work mode, she decided to wear it.

She also left her hair to fall free around her shoulders—the way she never, ever wore it on the job—and applied a touch more blush and mascara than usual.

"Holy cow! Look at you!" Seth said when he showed

up at the guesthouse with picnic basket in hand, ready to go.

"Too much?" she asked, gratified by his response but worrying again that she'd overdone it.

"Too much of what? You look great!" he assured her, his eyes going up and down her body as if he couldn't get enough.

And because of that Lacey opted to stay just the way she was.

The Founder's Day picnic festivities were held at the old covered bridge that was the town's namesake. It had been recently refurbished, and the entire area around it developed into a lush park.

There were games galore for the many kids in attendance and some for the adults, too. There were stands selling hot dogs, ice cream, snow cones, cotton candy, pretzels, funnel cakes and a number of other treats. There was a raffle for a motorcycle, a craft fair, and contests for the best the local cooks had to offer in the way of cakes, pies, and home-pickling of everything imaginable.

After a full afternoon taking it all in, Seth and Lacey did what everyone else did—they claimed a spot for themselves on the grassy knoll, spread out the blanket they'd brought and settled in to eat the picnic supper Seth had packed. Cold fried chicken and potato salad helped occupy them while they waited for darkness to fall and the fireworks display that promised to be more elaborate than the one on the Fourth of July had been.

"I can see why my brothers both love this town," Lacey told Seth, as they each sipped a glass of the wine he'd brought. "It's like one big family here, isn't it?"

"Yep," Seth confirmed.

"Lots of couples, though."

"Yep," he repeated.

"Cuts down on the possibilities of finding someone yourself if you're single, doesn't it?"

Lacey watched Seth's handsome face stretch into a slow, knowing grin. "Are you headed somewhere with this, Kincaid?"

She was, and since he'd been straightforward with his questions about her history with men the night before, Lacey shouldn't have been surprised that he would call her on her own beating around the bush.

But her curiosity had gotten the better of her, and she couldn't help it—the man was gorgeous, personable, fun to be with, sexy, successful, intelligent, kind and caring and even more, and she couldn't help wondering why he was single.

So she asked him point-blank.

"How come you're not married or engaged or with someone?"

"I'm right here with you," he said, as if she were missing the obvious, teasing her.

"You know what I mean."

Stretched out on his side on the blanket, dressed in jeans and a white Henley T-shirt, he was the very picture of relaxation. Before answering her he sat up, leaning most of his weight on one hip, his elbow braced on top of an upraised knee.

Then he shrugged a shoulder that filled out the Henley impeccably and looked her in the eye to answer. "You're right, small-town living isn't the best for dating—everybody knows everybody, if you haven't hit it off with anyone by the time you've been around the block a few times, you aren't going to find a whole lot more prospects in the pool."

"So you have dated people here?"

"Sure," he said. "Some really terrific women. Just not *the One*."

"And outside of Northbridge?" Lacey persisted.

"Sure," he repeated. "I've dated outside of North-bridge, too."

"And the One wasn't in either place?"

"Actually, the one I *thought* was the One was in both places—we met in Denver but I didn't date her there. Then I *did* start dating her when she came to North-bridge to get my computer network set up so I could run and monitor our other farms and ranches across the country from here."

Now they were getting somewhere…

"She was a computer techie?" Lacey asked.

"She was when I met her the first time in Denver. Two years later when she came here, she was the head of our whole computer division."

"She went from mere techie to head of the whole di-vision in only two years?"

"She was smart. And ambitious. Driven," he said emphatically. Lacey knew he was saying that she and this Charlotte person were alike in that way.

But it didn't seem like a compliment.

"Charlotte and I met when I was still working and living in Denver. A hacker got into my system and she had to come in to work on it. She and I had a few late nights working, sort of had a good time together, but that was it. Then I came here and needed a much bigger system set up. She said that when she saw the order, she decided to do it herself—even though by then she could have just sent another low-level techie."

"She came herself because she *liked* you," Lacey said, hoping to hide the flash of jealousy that had suddenly come out of nowhere.

"Yeah, that was pretty much what she said. But I liked her, too—we'd joked around and talked a lot when we were working together before. We had some things in common. But she *worked* for me, and you know how dicey that can be, so before she came here I'd figured I better not get into anything personal with her."

"Something here made it less dicey?"

"No, I knew it was still dicey. But...I don't know, things here seemed different somehow. More casual. Not so restricted. And Charlotte and I still had the same... I suppose you could say chemistry...that we'd had the first time around."

"So the second time the two of you crossed paths one thing led to another," Lacey said for him.

"Charlotte actually instigated things, so I sort of lost sight of the risks of getting involved with an employee and, yeah, one thing led to another."

"Don't tell me she ended up suing you for harassment or something."

"No, that wasn't Charlotte's style. But she definitely saw an opportunity to become part of the Camden family, and she wasn't about to let it pass her by."

"She became part of the family? You married her?" Lacey said with some shock. She'd never asked if he was divorced.

"No, it didn't get *that* far. She spent a lot of time here getting my system in working order and connecting it to what was being set up on each of the other farms around the country. By the time she'd finished, we were pretty hot and heavy, so we decided to try to keep it going long-distance. We did, for about eight months. Then we got engaged," he explained. "It was after that that things took a turn."

"How?"

Seth drank some of his wine, studied the glass for a moment and then said, "I knew Charlotte worked a lot—that was how she rose through the ranks as fast as she did. And I knew she was working a lot while she was in Denver and I was here, but I was under the impression that that was just how she kept herself busy because we weren't together."

"But it was more than that."

"Work was her priority. Everything—and *everyone*—took a backseat to that. And," he added in a voice filled with regret, "she wanted me to be more like that. More driven. More ambitious. More like she was. It didn't come out until after we were engaged, but she hated Northbridge, she hated country life. And she really, really hated that I'd handed over the CEO seat to Cade—"

"You were the CEO of Camden Incorporated and you handed it over to someone else?"

"My younger brother Cade," Seth confirmed. "As the oldest of the kids I stepped into it initially just by virtue of being the first of us to fully get on board with the company after college—it was how H.J. had it set up. He was determined that Camden Incorporated stay a family business. He arranged for us to have mentors he trusted, people to help us, advise us, but as each of us finished school and went to work, we went to work in a position of power. I was first, so I went in as head of everything."

"Only you didn't want that particular position of power—CEO."

"Right. I didn't want in on the business end of things—at least not any more than I have to be with the agricultural part of Camden Incorporated. Even though I knew I'd have to deal with business, I wanted that to be secondary to my working the ranch. So when Cade got his MBA and was ready to come on board, it just made more sense for him to become CEO so I could move here and do what I do."

"But Charlotte didn't approve of what you do?"

"She wanted me to *kick it into gear*—that's what she said. She figured my *rightful place* was as CEO, that together we could—and should—head the company."

"She was ambitious," Lacey marveled.

"Ambitious. She worked all the time. And I wasn't about to stage some sort of coup in my own family or become the business titan she thought I should become—which was really the only way she could respect me, she said. What it boiled down to was that the One was the Wrong One, and I broke it off with her."

"Oh, those *engagements,*" Lacey said, making a joke to lighten the dour tone that had developed. "Sometimes they bring out the worst in people."

Seth smiled, going along with her attempt at humor. "I guess we should be glad it was the engagements that brought out the worst in Charlotte and Dominic, and that we didn't end up married to them before we saw it."

"That would have been *much* worse," Lacey agreed.

"So that's how come I'm not married or engaged or with someone," he summed up.

"And why you're trying to corrupt my work ethic?" she teased.

He laughed and gave her a wicked wiggle of his eyebrows. "Yes. Ever since Charlotte I'm determined to corrupt every overworked girl I come across by forcing them to take a day off."

"Two days," she reminded.

"Two *half* days—that equals one day."

"Still, it's corrupting me because I'm not looking forward to going back to work tomorrow."

"Then don't," he enticed.

Lacey laughed. "The training center won't build itself."

Dusk had fallen as they'd talked. On the other side of the creek running below the bridge, music suddenly blared from a loudspeaker, accompanied by a voice that announced, "The Founder's Day Light Show!"

Which Lacey thought was good timing, because clearly talking about how the One had turned into the Wrong One for Seth was a subject better left in the dust.

Except for one more small thing she was curious about.

As he moved to sit beside her so he could see the fireworks, she swayed in his direction and whispered, "Where is Charlotte now?"

"Long gone—she left for a bigger and better job with a software company in New Zealand."

New Zealand.

Far, far away, Lacey thought.

And for some reason that made her particularly happy.

* * *

"I can see a clock that's stopped from here—looks like the power has been out since about half an hour after we left this afternoon," Seth said, as he unlocked one set of the French doors on the main house. Then he opened them and a gust of hot air flooded out. "Woo! Feels like it, too! It's a blast furnace in there!"

They'd both noticed as they'd neared his ranch on the drive home that the streetlights weren't lit. None of the outdoor lights around the houses, the pool and the garage were on when they drove around to park in front of the garage door that wouldn't operate without the electric garage door opener. And now it was clear that the houses that were ordinarily air-conditioned had retained the August heat through the entire afternoon and evening.

Seth took out his cell phone and called the utility company in town. After a few minutes of listening, he reported to Lacey that the power would be out until approximately eleven.

"Why don't we open windows to let some of the heat out," he suggested, "and meet back here to sit by the pool while we wait for the air to come on again? That bottle of wine we started is still pretty full."

It *was* barely ten o'clock, and Lacey knew she wouldn't be able to sleep until the guesthouse was cool again. Not to mention that she wasn't about to pass up any excuse to extend her time with Seth.

"No, I guess we shouldn't let that wine go to waste," she said by way of agreement.

Seth smiled at her. "I'll meet you back here then," he repeated.

As Seth went into the main house Lacey rounded

the pool and unlocked the door to the swelteringly hot guesthouse.

She made a quick tour of the place to throw open every window, then took a fast look in the bathroom mirror to see how her appearance had fared through the day.

There had been a breeze most of the time that had diffused the heat while they were out, so she hadn't done too badly: her mascara had kept its promise and not smudged or smeared, her blush might have been gone but her cheeks were sun-kissed and now had a healthy, more natural look to them.

She did brush her hair to make it fluffy and full again, reapply lip gloss and kick off her sandals so she could be in bare feet. But her sundress still looked fresh as a daisy, the fabric was light and filmy, and the halter top with its plunging neckline left her as cool as anything she could change into, so she let the dress stay, too.

Then she hurried out of the hot house and back into the cooler evening air.

Seth wasn't there yet. The clean, clear water of the pool beckoned, so she bunched up the skirt of her dress to hold high on her thighs, sat poolside and dangled her feet into the water.

"We could swim."

The sound of Seth's voice made her smile. She glanced up to see him coming out of the main house with the wine and two glasses in hand.

He'd stayed in his jeans and Henley T-shirt but now his feet were bare, too—free of the cowboy boots he'd been wearing before.

"I thought about swimming," Lacey admitted. "But I was just feeling too lazy."

He'd shaved. She didn't notice that until he smiled, but he'd grown a bit scruffy as the day and evening had gone on and now that scruff was gone, replaced by smooth, whisker-free skin and the scent of his cologne.

He joined her after pouring the wine, handed her one of the glasses then sat beside her. Not so his feet could go into the water, though. He sat facing her, his legs crossed, his own wineglass held in both hands.

"You look a little lazy—I like it," he said after a sip.

"Corruption complete?"

"Are you going back to work tomorrow?" he challenged.

"Of course."

"Then you're not *completely* corrupted, are you?"

Lacey answered that with a smile. "Still, this has been really nice—this whole *winding down* thing you speak so highly of," she said, emphasizing the phrase as if it were a foreign concept.

"And you're good at it, too. I'm glad to see that—it means there's hope for you after all."

"I'm not sure what there's hope for, but I wouldn't want to be considered hopeless," Lacey said with a laugh after sipping her own wine.

"Hopeless—like Charlotte, for instance—would have involved you being on the Internet or your phone every minute of these last two days and barely humoring me. But you didn't do that."

"I didn't think that was part of the deal."

"It wasn't. But that wouldn't have stopped Charlotte."

"Points for me, demerits for her."

Seth laughed as he drank more wine. "Nothin' but demerits for her. But you earned a lot of points," he said in a voice rife with insinuation.

"Enough points to buy a road?"

"Next week—we're not talking about that until you've given me the whole weekend. And there's two hours to go on that."

"I just have to fill two hours and then it's back to business?" she asked with some insinuation of her own, even though she wasn't sure where it had come from or what she was insinuating.

"Yep, two hours. Have anything in mind?"

She had something in mind instantly.

For Lacey, what had ignited between them at the end of the previous evening had been simmering just below the surface ever since. So certainly now, in the quiet of the night, sitting beside the pool with nothing but moonlight and the glimmer of stars reflected in the water, it didn't take more than insinuation for thoughts of kissing, of touching, of making love to spring back to life.

But she wasn't going to say that outright.

"Do you have anything in mind?" she countered, knowing she shouldn't bait him and yet suddenly also knowing exactly how she wanted this night, this weekend, this down time to end. Exactly what would be the perfect finish…

"Wasn't me who stopped things last night," Seth said. "Seems like it shouldn't be me who starts them up again."

But he did dip forward to kiss the very tip of her shoulder and while that seemed innocent, it was still enough to get things rolling for Lacey.

Why had she stopped them the night before? she asked herself.

Because she'd thought that if she hadn't stopped, she would have risked everything.

But now, in the peace and calm of the evening, after two days of relaxing and recharging, she wondered what was really at risk. Would she not go back to work tomorrow morning if she had this night with Seth? she reasoned. Would she not build the training facility?

Of course she would go back to work; of course she would build the center. One night wouldn't—couldn't—change that.

So there wasn't really anything at risk.

Last night had just been jitters, she thought. And tonight she wasn't feeling jittery. She was still feeling the way she had been when she'd put on that dress this morning—feminine and free to do as she pleased.

"Too hot inside," she said in a seductress's voice.

"Nice out here, though," he answered quietly.

"Where anyone could see?"

"There's not another soul for miles." He kissed her shoulder again, moving up an inch nearer to her neck and lingering a bit longer. "But it's up to you."

Laccy could feel her nipples tightening against the soft drape of the dress. And almost on its own, her free hand rose to the first button of his Henley shirt and unfastened it.

Seth looked down at her hand and as he got the message she was sending, he smiled again. "You sure?"

Lacey undid the second button and made him laugh.

"Hang on," he said, getting to his feet in one lithe movement and disappearing into the main house.

Nothing about him had changed when he returned scant minutes later. Lacey had taken her feet from the water to place them flat on the poolside tile and pulled the skirt of her dress over her upraised knees.

"If you went in to turn on a video camera this is a no-go," she warned.

He laughed as he sat back down. "Protection," he said simply. "Unless you're against it."

"No, protection is good," she said.

And so was the first meeting of his mouth and hers when he leaned forward to kiss her. Very good.

He stretched out his legs on either side of her, took her by the ankles and pulled her toward him, draping her thighs over his. He let his forearms rest on his calves as he continued kissing her.

They were off to a slow start, which was just the way it seemed like things should be. Lacey's eyes closed so she could drift completely into the simple joy of that kiss.

In no hurry at all, his lips parted; he waited for hers to catch up. Then his tongue, tempting and sweet, brought mischief into the game, turning the kiss playful and coy.

As their heads tilted, the kiss inched its way toward intensity. Seth raised the back of his hand to her cheek, smoothing her hair away from her face, then he rested that hand along the side of her neck.

And yet the leisurely pace didn't matter. Anticipation mounted in Lacey anyway, and she was again very aware of her breasts, her nipples, striving for his attention.

She unfastened the remaining three buttons of his shirt. And with that done, it seemed silly to leave it on, so she found the hem and rolled it up his broad back to pull over his head and off during a split-second break from that kiss.

She tossed his shirt aside and ran her flattened palms from his sides to his washboard belly, up to impeccable pectorals, across to biceps built from hard ranch work, and up and over massive shoulders to that back that was cut and carved and gave her a wealth of hills and valleys to explore.

Just the feel of him was enough to light sparks in her blood. He was honed and taut, silky-smooth and strong.

And he liked what she was doing to him. She knew because his mouth was open even wider over hers, their kisses becoming deeper and deeper with every slide of her hands, his tongue more assertive and demanding.

His hands came away from her face, from her neck. He bracketed her hips, pulling her closer—not quite against him, not quite into the very V of his legs, but near to it. And when he'd finished with that he reached around her neck to the bow that kept the halter dress in place and slowly untied it.

Lacey's dress slipped down to form mere clouds of fabric dangling from pebbled nipples, and she felt the breath of evening air tickle the very top curves of her areolas.

Seth began a trail of kisses down her neck and along her collarbone to the hollow in front of her shoulder. From there the trail led farther south until it was his lips only faintly, lightly kissing that upper shadow of nipple.

The feeling was powerful, and it caused her breasts to heave forward, sending one side of her dress to fall completely away.

It was that exposed breast that Seth covered with a big, warm hand before he recaptured her mouth with an all-new fervor in a kiss that was hungry and demanding.

What had come alive in Lacey the previous evening was nothing compared to what was awakening now. Every nerve ending seemed on the surface of her skin, feeding sensations like tinder to the flames beginning to burn inside of her.

She answered his kiss with an urgency of her own as her hands coursed across his back, his shoulders, his chest and belly all over again.

And when she reached the waistband of his jeans she didn't even pause before she unfastened the button and unzipped the zipper, freeing his own burgeoning desire.

With his arms around her, Seth eased her back on the tile and stretched out next to her.

The other side of her dress came away with that movement. Again he broke the kiss and dropped his head to the other breast.

He drew her into his hot, moist mouth. Lacey's spine arched in response as his tongue flicked the crystallized crest, circled and taunted it, idolized and adored it, and worked her into a frenzy of need greater than she was sure she could bear.

He rolled them both to their sides, then reached around to unzip her dress, finally ridding her of it. This left her in only lace bikini panties. He abandoned her for a moment to shed his jeans and whatever else he had on underneath them.

Her quick glimpse of him through the French doors Saturday night had not prepared her for the pure masculine beauty of his naked body in all its glory, and seeing it now lit even more flames inside of her.

Magnificent and all man—he was lean and tight and rippling with muscle—and once he'd removed her panties and quickly sheathed himself, she was only too happy to be able to greet naked flesh with naked flesh when he came to her again.

Their mouths met once more, as Seth retook her breasts with big, adept hands.

Lacey took something of his, too, reaching low and discovering just what a frenzy she could raise in him, as well.

A gravelly rumble of a groan sounded from his throat and he once again moved his mouth to her breast. Tongue and teeth did a delightful torment of her nipple, and his hand slid down her stomach and between her legs.

Her breath caught at that first touch, at the fabulous fingers that brought her close enough to the brink to make her nearly beg him for more.

And that was when he part-rolled, part-eased them both into the pool, into the shallow end where the water was as warm as a bath.

But swimming was not what he had in mind.

Before Lacey could say anything, his mouth was over hers again and with her back against the smooth tiles of the pool's sidewall, he brought her legs up to wrap them around his hips and entered her in one sublime slide that fitted them together as if that was how they were meant to be.

A small sneak preview of a climax rippled through Lacey at just that moment. Her head arched backward as a gust of breath was stolen from her.

Then he moved deeper into her and showed her that there was so much more to come.

Lacey held on as he pressed fully, completely, into her, as he pulled slightly out again. In and out. Again. And again, until together they devised a rhythm of meeting and parting, of flowing with the movement they were creating in the water, rising and falling with it, striving, striving, striving for that ultimate of peaks.

The climax that broke over the two of them at the same time had them holding tight to each other as he embedded himself so deeply within her that Lacey felt as if he truly was a part of her core, of her being, sealing them together with wave after wave of an ecstasy so divine she lost herself to it, in it.

Tiny sounds emitted from her throat, and she could do nothing but cling to him until little by little the pure glory of it ebbed, slowly, slowly draining her until she wilted against him and trusted that he would brace and support her there while he, too, came down from that pillar of pleasure.

Lacey's head fell to his chest. His face dropped to her hair. And she could feel his breath hot and heavy there as they stayed wrapped in the pure afterglow, his strong arms around her, keeping her braced as the surface of the water calmed to glass again.

"It never—*ever*—occurred to me that *this* might be the way I got into this pool for the first time," she whispered when she'd gathered her wits.

Seth laughed a raspy, ragged laugh. "Kinda nice, though, wasn't it?"

So much more than *kinda nice*...

"I'm not complaining," she assured him, tightening her legs around him and getting a tiny aftershock that reminded her just how nice it had been.

"How 'bout hurtin'—you aren't doing any of that, either, are you?"

"I'm definitely feeling no pain," she answered with a smile.

He lifted her then and came away from her, repositioning them so he could scoop her into his arms and carry her to the stairs at the corner of the pool.

Climbing the steps, he took her to one of the over-sized loungers and laid her there. Then he joined her and pulled her to lie conformed to his side where the heat of his body, of his arms around her, chased away the slight chill of the night air on her bare, wet skin.

"Still no lights, so it's probably too hot to go inside," he said, sounding weighted and weary. "Guess we'll have to stay out here… Maybe take another dip in the pool in a little while…"

Lacey laughed, but she didn't contradict him. It was just too wonderful to be there with him, like that, under the canopy of stars.

And the possibility of doing again what they'd just done was not something she could deny herself. Not when nothing had ever felt as good or as right as that had.

And not when there wasn't a single other thought in her head but being with this man….

Chapter Ten

After the most amazing night Seth had ever had with anyone, he spent the next five days as nothing more than an unhappy spectator in Lacey's overworked week.

They'd had all of Sunday night together. When the power and air-conditioning had come back on they'd moved into his bedroom where they'd made love, slept, made love, slept, made love again. And again on Monday morning, when Lacey had been no more eager than he had been to leave his bed and rejoin the world.

But since then Seth had been relegated to watching her from the main house.

He saw her leave each morning when he was barely rolling out of bed at dawn. And despite the fact that he'd waited up and watched for her to come home each and every night, there had been another night like the one the week before when she hadn't made it home at all, and on the other three nights she'd dragged herself back so late and looking so tired that he'd thought the kindest thing he could do was just keep his distance and let her get to bed. Alone.

Twice he'd thought there was a chance to spend some time with her when her assistant had called to arrange for him to go to the construction site for a meeting about the road she wanted to put through his property.

Both times he'd imagined getting her alone for an hour, maybe sneaking up to the old house's attic.

But her assistant had called to reschedule the first appointment, and when he'd arrived at the site for the second one her assistant had apologized but said that Lacey had had to rush out to the scene of an accident that had caused an injury to one of her crew, canceling that meeting before it could happen, too.

What it all added up to, he told himself on Friday night as he showered after his own day's work, was to more and more proof of why he should just write this whole thing off. Why he should resist his attraction to her. It was evidence right there in front of him of just how driven she was, of what was most important to her, of how obsessed she was.

Just the way his own father had been.

Just the way Charlotte had been.

Work, work, work. First. Foremost. Forever.

And even worse with Lacey was the fact that for her it wasn't only about the work or the drive to succeed, the way it had been for Charlotte. For Lacey there was that personal element, that determination she had to prove something to her father. To compete with her brothers for Morgan Kincaid's respect.

So if he had any brains at all, Seth told himself, he

would just forget about Lacey and get on with things the way they'd been before he'd ever set eyes on her.

But the truth was, he wanted her, and he wanted her bad.

He ached for her. He burned for her. He couldn't stop thinking about her. He couldn't stop reliving in his mind their night together. He couldn't stop plotting and planning and trying to figure out a way to have some time with her—hell, he'd lost hours and hours of sleep this week just to catch a glimpse of her out his window when she was coming or going.

And none of that had been true with Charlotte.

He'd been crazy about Charlotte. He had. But somehow his feelings for her hadn't had the same kind of intensity as the ones he had for Lacey. Maybe that was why things with Charlotte hadn't really popped when he'd first met her in Denver. Why it had been so easy for him to keep it strictly business until later, when she'd come here.

But with Lacey? Things had popped the day they'd first met, from the minute he'd seen her walking across that open field in her high heels.

Finished rinsing away the soap and shampoo, he turned off the spray of water, closed his eyes, hung his head and shook it in disbelief of himself, of what he was thinking, feeling.

He couldn't stop wanting her. Craving just a glance from those beautiful green eyes. The touch of her hand. The silkiness of her hair falling across his skin.

He couldn't stop the images of them sharing a future together. The images of her sharing his bed every night. Waking up with him every morning. Having his kids. Spending the rest of their lives together.

Opening his eyes again, he reached for the towel slung over the shower door and began to dry off, wondering as he did what the hell was wrong with him. Telling himself to just let everything with Lacey go. To get over her before it went any further.

But the first thing he did when he finally stepped out of the shower stall and opened the bathroom window to let the steam out was crane around to catch the sliver of a view he got of the guesthouse to see if she might have gotten home while he'd been showering.

No, no lights.

Of course not, he thought. It was only a little past nine. And so what if it was Friday night? To someone like Lacey, Friday was just another workday; it wasn't the end of the week. She was probably planning to work Saturday and Sunday, too. He probably wouldn't be able to get any time with her then, either.

Just give it up....

Except that even as he dispensed that bit of advice to himself, he knew he couldn't. Last weekend had hooked him.

Because last weekend had been great. Even before they'd ended up making love in the pool. And it was the ways that Lacey was unlike Charlotte that had really sucked him in.

Because unlike Charlotte, Lacey could—and had—left work behind completely once she'd had her mornings to accomplish something. She could—and had—slowed down and enjoyed things besides work. And when she did, when she had, he'd lost sight of the workaholic in her, lost sight of everything *but* her. And then he'd fallen for her.

So why, if she could do it last weekend, couldn't she do it on a regular basis? he thought.

After all, Charlotte couldn't—or wouldn't—have done last weekend the way Lacey had. If he was re-membering right, his father wouldn't have, either. His father would have worked, too, and left Seth's mother to spend time with the kids.

But now Seth knew that there was a part of Lacey that *wasn't* a workaholic. Now he knew that she could be persuaded to set work aside. And that once she had, she could enjoy not working.

And as long as that part of her existed, couldn't he keep tapping into it?

Not without some effort, he knew.

But when the effort paid off it was so worth it, that maybe he was willing to keep doing whatever it took.

It wouldn't be easy under the overriding shadow of her father and that determination she had to prove her-self. To have a position with the family business that was as important as his sons had held. But easy didn't matter as much to him as having Lacey did, he realized.

It also didn't help that he'd already relegated himself to some kind of nonentity because he wasn't a huge foot-ball fan, or that Lacey could be relegated to that same nonentity status if she was with him.

So what if he became a football fan? he asked him-self, still trying to fix things so he could have her.

He knew the game. The teams. Enough about the major players. A little more in-depth reading of the sports page, a little studying up on the subject, a little updating himself on Morgan Kincaid's contribution, stats, history, and he'd be able to hold his own with the former football star.

That was something small that he was willing to do if it meant he wouldn't be a detriment to Lacey. If it meant that she could feel better about being with him.

And it wasn't something she'd asked of him—that occurred to him as he shaved. That he'd come up with it on his own was important.

Because also unlike Charlotte, Lacey didn't want him to be something he wasn't. She didn't want to change him. She didn't disapprove of him or think she should turn him into another version of her. So doing something like showing more interest in football for her sake—when it was his own decision, when it wasn't a demand she was making of him, when it didn't entail changing who he was—was no big deal.

But really, wasn't that how he was leaning all the way around? If they each could just bend a little—if Lacey could just back off of work slightly, if he could show more of an interest in the sport that drove her family, then couldn't they meet in the middle and have something together?

Maybe he was kidding himself, but in that moment when all he wanted was to find any way to be with her, to have her, when he wanted to see her, to hear her voice, to touch her and kiss her and take her in his arms so much it had him tied in knots, he thought they could.

And he knew he had to at least talk to her about it. Give it his best shot.

Because he wanted her too much not to.

And nothing he did, nothing he told himself, nothing at all, could shut that feeling down.

"Dad, are you hearing what you're saying?" Lacey couldn't believe she was sitting at her desk at ten on Friday night having this phone call with her father. "I've just told you that we made up half the work that didn't get done last week and that by the end of next week we will have made up the rest. That means that at the end of week three, we will be where we're scheduled to be even though we lost all of week one. And you're *still* not happy?"

"*Ahead* of schedule! What have I always said? Just being good enough isn't good enough! Under budget and ahead of schedule—that's what you should be shooting for."

"Well, it helps the budget that we're getting three weeks' worth of work done in two weeks—*without* paying overtime. Right now that's all I can tell you." And she'd foolishly thought that that might please him, which was why she'd called to report to him.

"Don't you go paying overtime without getting my okay!"

"We aren't paying overtime, Dad—that's what I said. You've already made your position clear on the subject—it isn't something I've forgotten." And oh boy, was she sorry she'd called him. "I won't keep you," she said then, to at least cut short her mistake. "I just thought I'd give you an update. I'll talk to you next week."

"Did you get that road worked out with Camden?" her father demanded instead of letting her off the phone.

Camden.

Seth.

Just his name sent a wave of longing through her.

"We haven't worked out the details yet. I tried to do that twice this last week but couldn't get to it. Maybe this weekend…"

"Don't tell me you're taking this weekend off to

spend with him! If I can't get things done because you're being googly-eyed over some man—"

"I'm not taking this weekend off. And if I talk to Seth about the road, that's work, isn't it? It's what you just *told* me to get done." It was time to end this call before her father could tear into her any more. "It's late so I'm going to let you go. If anything happens with the road I'll call."

"Don't you let him pull any Camden shenanigans on us, little girl," her father said suspiciously.

"I won't," she assured him, rather than saying anything else that might prolong this. "Good night, Dad."

Her father finally said good-night, and Lacey got to hang up.

Then she let her head drop to her desk.

Would her father ever think she was good enough? Would any job she did meet his standards? She knew how hard he'd always been on Ian and Hutch, but somehow it seemed like he was being even more unreasonable with her.

Naturally she knew he would say that she thought he was being more unreasonable because—like all women—she was overly sensitive and couldn't take what a man could take…

She drew in a deep breath and sighed it out. Then she sat up again, intending to get back to work.

Which was when she thought she might be hallucinating. Looking through the archway that connected her dining-room office with the old house's living room and out the picture window, she thought she saw Seth's truck coming down the road.

She blinked and kept watching, trying not to get too excited, telling herself that it could be any one of a dozen people who drove to work out there every day in white trucks.

Except that no one would be coming back to work now.

The truck pulled up to the front of the house, and she could see Seth behind the wheel. That first sight of him wiped away her exhaustion.

Cowboy boots, jeans, a cream-colored dress shirt—that's what she saw him wearing as he got out of the truck once he'd stopped the engine.

Nothing and no one had ever looked so good to her.

Too good for her to care why he might be there or that her own tan twill slacks and red crewneck T-shirt were hardly alluring, or that her ponytail could have become lopsided during her long, long day.

The only thing that registered was that Seth was on his way up the porch steps.

Lacey stood and went around her desk, calling "Come in!" in answer to his knock on the front door. It was only when she met him in the entryway that it finally struck her that regardless of how intimate they'd been when she'd left him on Monday morning, she hadn't so much as caught a glimpse of him since then and maybe she should curb the inclination to throw herself into his arms.

As if she needed something to anchor her to keep from doing that, she wrapped a nonchalant elbow around the newel post at the foot of the stairs to the second floor and said, "This is a surprise."

Seth didn't even say hello. He merely crossed the entry and did what she'd had in mind—he took her by the shoulders, pulled her to him and kissed her as if nothing had separated last weekend and now. Deeply, intensely, profoundly, soundly, thoroughly, he kissed her. And while Lacey attempted to keep up and give as good as she got, some of that kiss just swept her off her feet, leaving her slightly light-headed when he ended it, let go of her and took half a step backward.

Luckily Lacey still had hold of the newel post to keep herself on her feet.

"That was some kind of hello," she said with a laugh.

"It barely scratches the surface," he countered in a voice that was lower than usual, that seemed to mean business—although Lacey wasn't sure why that thought occurred to her.

"I've been watching you coming and going all week—when you actually *did* come and go," he said.

"Tuesday night I fell asleep at my desk again. It's still been crazy, but I gained a little ground to make up for our slow start, so—"

"Do not say it was worth it," he warned.

"I was going to say *so that was good.*"

"That was the only good thing about this week, then," he muttered, then said, "That's why I'm here—I want to do something about it."

Lacey was confused, and it must have shown in her expression because he went on before she'd said anything, telling her about how he'd hoped each and every night that she might get home early enough to spend some time with him, how he'd hoped every morning that she might hang around long enough to come and have breakfast with him, how he'd even fantasized about the meetings she'd missed turning into more than business meetings.

"And after all that, I started out tonight telling myself to forget it," he said. "To forget last weekend. To forget any hope that we might have any portion of that again. To forget you."

Lacey was still glad to be holding the newel post because she'd begun to wonder if he'd come here to end whatever it was that was going on between them. And even though she didn't fully understand it, she was struck hard by that thought. Hard enough to need some support to go on facing him if that was what she was in store for.

"So what was that entrance you just made—one last kiss to say goodbye?" she asked, hating that her voice sounded so apprehensive.

He shook his head. "I just wanted you to remember what things are like between us before I say what I came to say."

Things between them were amazing. Remarkable. Incredible. She'd missed him and wanted him so much this past week that it had been awful never even seeing him. She'd relived every moment of their weekend together, of their night of lovemaking a million times in her mind. She'd wanted nothing more than to get home earlier each night and maybe spend it with him. She'd looked over at the main house on her way out every morning, tempted to delay her day, to have even a few minutes with him.

So the kiss had been great, but she hadn't needed it or anything else to remind her of this man.

"What did you come to say?" she asked hesitantly, worrying that he wanted her to know what she'd be missing when he told her they were through.

"That even though I told myself to forget you, I came out on the other end of that—not only can't I forget you,

I think we have something, Lacey. Something I want. Something that I'm willing to work on to have."

"I'm not sure what that means—"

"I'll tell you what it means."

He did just that, telling her how much he'd missed her and wanted her. How much he wanted her to be a part of his life—not merely a passing-through part, but a very real, very permanent part. The primary part. He went on to say words that she began to hang on because the picture he painted of them together, of a future together, was so appealing.

"I'll even become the biggest football fan of them all," he said as he drew to a close. "In a room full of football players and fanatics, I'll make sure I'm the one your father wants to talk football with. I guarantee that I won't drag you down. I'll be your greatest asset, not the drawback that other guy was. All I want is for you to meet me halfway."

"I'll never get my father to tone down the football stuff even halfway, if that's what you mean. Football is what runs in his veins."

"That's not what I mean. I want you to meet me halfway by putting some limits on the work you do so your hours are reasonable and we can be together."

"Put some limits on work?" she repeated with a facetious sort of chuckle. "Do you think I wouldn't have done that already if I could have? I'm putting in the hours I need to put in to get the jobs done—for the training center and the sportswear line. As it is, I'm barely keeping up. Doing the smallest amount less would put me behind."

"Then let's find a way to fix that," he said. "I've thought about it and I'm figuring there isn't much wiggle room with the clothing line. But when it comes to the training center, I think there are some options."

"You're kidding."

"I know what it means to you that your father gave you this project. But it's too much. What you're having to do by yourself is unreasonable. So what if you take another look at it? See if you can extend some dead-lines—"

"That isn't possible. My father wants this facility open in the spring. Or earlier—he wants me *ahead* of schedule, not extending the schedule."

"Okay, then what about including Ian again, sharing the load?"

"My father took Ian *off* the project."

"Because your father was angry about what went on with the property issue—but surely by now he's cooled down. I saw him at the wedding, at the groundbreaking—he and Ian seem to be on fine terms. And now that the project is underway, now that all the problems with acquiring the property are ironed out—"

"Not *all* the property problems are ironed out. There's still the access road we need."

"Anything you need, Lacey—that's what I'll give you. Anything, any way you need it, if you'll just work with me on this. Your father doesn't seem at odds with Ian now—negotiate getting Ian back on the project, doing it jointly with him."

"I might as well just buy a billboard that announces that I can't do the job."

"You *can* do the job, but do you want to do it at the expense of everything else? I'm just asking you to do it in more moderation so we can have a life, too. If you *choose* to share the load and make your father see that it's a choice, not a necessity, that it's something you're opting for in order to have a life of your own, isn't that a position you can take?"

"The only way I can prove that I can do the job is to do it. Myself. Without asking for concessions or help or extensions."

"Then what about just *not* doing it?" Seth said.

"Just *not* doing it?" she parroted in disbelief.

"What's the worst that would happen if you said *to hell* with it all, with proving your father wrong, *to hell* with whatever role your father put you in, *to hell* with everything but just doing what you want, what makes you happy? Because from where I'm sitting, I'm wondering why—if what you really enjoy doing is sportswear—why go on with this project at all? Why not hand it back to your father, focus on the clothing line, have a life with me and forget the rest."

"I'll tell you why!" Lacey said, her temper flaring in the face of what seemed like Seth discounting her goals the same way Dominic had. "The training center is my chance. The only chance I've been given to step up and do what *I* know I can do. To grab the brass ring, if that's how you want to look at it. That's first and foremost. I've worked for this opportunity, *fought* for it. I'm not just going to shrug my shoulders at it now, slip away and be *your* little woman!"

She had a full head of steam and she couldn't contain it.

"And besides that," she shouted, "to say that poor-little-me can't do the job would mean that my father won every fight I've ever had with him, that he was right—that no matter what a woman says, she ends up focusing on a man, a family, *clothes!* He'd say he was right not to trust me with anything important before this. Not to trust any woman with anything important because the minute a man comes on the scene, that's where she ends up."

"So what? So what if he says that? If he believes it? In the long run, what difference does it actually make? Is it better to prove a point than to be happy? I saw a new you last weekend, a relaxed Lacey, a happier Lacey when you were out from under your father's thumb for a while, and you can't tell me otherwise."

She could, but it wouldn't have been true. She *had* been a more relaxed version of herself with Seth last weekend. She had enjoyed it and felt good about it and hated having it come to an end.

But that one weekend didn't change the fact that now that she had this opportunity with Kincaid Corporation, she couldn't just throw it away. And to do anything but handle it all herself, all by herself, was to throw it away because she knew that to bring Ian in would mean Ian would get the credit.

"So you'll become a football fanatic, and in return for that you think I should give up building the training center," she said.

"All I'm asking," Seth said, interrupting her thoughts, "is just that you go at a different pace. A more human pace. That you do whatever it takes to end your workday sometime before midnight, that you take weekends off, so we can have some time together."

"I can do my job, but at *your* pace, the way you want me to do it," she said, unable to see how this could end well.

He reached to take her arms again, but something in Lacey made her step backward, out of that reach.

"What I want," he said slowly, enunciating each word, "is you. Time *with* you. A life *with* you. And I want you to do what you want to do, but I think that this *pace* you keep and your determination to make this point with your father is keeping you from admitting what you *do* want—even to yourself. Because just maybe what you *do* want is what your father thought you might end up wanting."

"Really? Is that so?" she said sarcastically, hating that he was telling her about herself as if he knew more than she did, telling her that her father was right, pushed buttons he shouldn't push. "You're so convinced that what I want is you and being your *little* woman, and maybe doing some token job to keep me busy."

"No, that's not what I said. I want us to have a life together and for that to come first for us both. And no, I can't be sure that's what you want. I can only hope it might be. What I *am* saying is that maybe you can't be sure, either, because you're so intent on competing and proving your point that you haven't thought beyond the damn training center and making your damn point with your father. That even if it creeps in just slightly—like last weekend—you push aside what actually *does* make you happy, what you just might want, and go back to burying yourself under that drive to show your old man that you're as good as his sons."

"What I want," Lacey said, enunciating each word the way he had, "is what I'm doing."

He studied her for a long moment before he said, "This might be easier if I thought that was true. But I think you'd deny what you actually do want rather than let your father be right. And at the end of that you just lose, Lacey. You lose by your own hand and I'm not sure you see that." He shook his head, his voice went low and gravelly, and he added, "The trouble is, I lose, too. But you aren't going to let me do anything about that, are you?"

This was definitely falling apart, and inside, so was Lacey.

But she swallowed back the tears that filled her throat and whispered, "I guess not."

He shook his head again—this time in disgust—then he turned and went out the way he'd come in.

And Lacey stayed frozen where she was, chin high, hanging on for dear life to that newel post until she heard the sound of Seth's truck far in the distance.

Then she slid down the post, feeling the heat of salty tears sting her eyes and trail to her jawbone.

And she told herself that she'd just done the only thing she could have done.

No matter how bad it felt.

Chapter Eleven

Lacey just worked.

All of the weekend that followed her breakup with Seth, all of the next week, Saturday and Sunday of the weekend after that, and even until four in the afternoon on Labor Day, she threw herself more into work than she ever had before.

Day and night—overseeing every tiny detail of the construction of the Monarchs' training center, and managing every aspect of her clothing line's production, marketing, sales, distribution and website over the phone and via the Internet—she worked. She barely slept more than three or four hours a night, and she'd spent those three or four hours on an air mattress she put upstairs in the old house, near the functioning bathroom.

It was only on Labor Day that she took her first real break. And she might not have done that except that Hutch was back from his honeymoon and both of her brothers had threatened to roll her in a rug and carry her if need be to Ian and Jenna's Labor Day barbecue.

So Lacey had a plan: if she was going to be forced to take time off, she was going to catch up on a few non-work things that she'd let lapse.

She would attend the barbecue from four until seven or eight o'clock that evening.

Then she'd drop some things at the furnished apartment in the upper floor of the house-turned-duplex that Hutch owned—the apartment that she'd again arranged with Hutch to use after her falling-out with Seth, but had yet to manage to move into.

At the apartment she would take a hot shower—a luxury, since the ancient shower she'd been using at the old house-slash-office was rarely more than lukewarm.

She would also wash and condition her hair.

Then she would bide her time with more paperwork until 1:00 or 2:00 a.m., when she could be reasonably sure that Seth would be sound asleep.

During the middle of that first Friday night she'd gone to the Camden ranch, made sure there were no lights on in the main house, then slipped into the guest-house to pack a bag with just enough to tide her over. She'd sent her assistant to pack up her business-related things during the following week. But there were still some personal things that needed to be retrieved. So, at 1:00 or 2:00 a.m. she would finish off her Labor Day hiatus by finally and completely clearing her things out of his guesthouse.

And after that she would go back to the office for another night on the air mattress so she could start the next week at the crack of dawn.

Because working like a fiend was the only chance

she had of outrunning the misery that overwhelmed her every time a thought of Seth crept in, so it was important that any window of time that opened up be planned, filled and kept a tight rein on.

Which was what she had every intention of doing with her first dreaded downtime since the Founder's Day weekend she'd spent so blissfully with Seth...

"Oh, my gosh, you look *awful!*"

Lacey could tell that her new sister-in-law hadn't meant to greet her like that when she first opened her front door, because Jenna turned a bright shade of red and quickly followed with "I'm sorry! That came out wrong. Of course you don't look *awful,* just tired. I can see why Ian and Hutch are worried about you. Come in, come in."

Lacey went into the farmhouse her brother Ian now shared with Jenna and Abby and waved a hello to her even newer sister-in-law, Issa, who was watching from the kitchen at the end of the hallway.

"Yacey!"

Lacey's nearly three-year-old nephew Ash couldn't pronounce her name. *Yacey* was his version, and he shouted it as he charged her to wrap his arms around her knees.

"Hi, babycakes. How's my guy?" Lacey greeted him, bending over to give him a hug.

"We gots marshallows to cook later," he confided.

"Marshmallows," Jenna translated. "For s'mores."

"I can't wait," Lacey said to them all, faking enthusiasm and energy she didn't have.

Then Ash let go of her knees and reached for her hand. "I'm s'posa bring you out the back," he said, as if he'd been given a very important mission.

"Ian and Hutch are out there," Jenna explained.

"Is there something I can do in here to help first?" Lacey offered.

Jenna shook her head as if it were unthinkable. "No, no, go with Ash."

Lacey had the sense that something was going on, but she gave in and let her nephew lead her through the farmhouse and out the back door, where her brothers were sitting on two of three folding chairs.

They greeted her as Ash drew her all the way to the third folding chair and ordered her to sit. Then Hutch said to his son, "Go play with Abby now, Ash."

"'Cuz you gotta talk to Yacey," Ash said, echoing something he'd heard.

"What is this, an intervention?" Lacey asked with a laugh when Ash trotted off in the direction of the sandbox.

"Sort of," Hutch answered with a laugh of his own.

"No, not sort of," Ian corrected. "This is definitely an intervention. We're worried about you."

Jenna had told her that. Apparently it was a subject of discussion.

"Nobody needs to worry about me, I'm fine," Lacey assured them in an airy tone that sounded fake even to her own ears.

"Oh, come on, Lace, that's not true," Hutch cajoled. "You said you didn't want to stay at the Camden ranch after all and wanted to use the apartment. But Issa and I are still living downstairs until we move next month, remember? I know you haven't been there a single night since you said that—"

"And my assistant talked to your assistant when she called to find out where the copy of that first land survey was," Ian interjected. "We know you're *sleeping* at the construction site."

Was that *all* they knew? Had they heard or pieced together anything about her and Seth?

It didn't seem as though they could have, so she said, "We've had a rough start and I've been trying to make up time. Plus I'm dealing with my sportswear, don't forget. Sleeping at the office is just a temporary thing for convenience. There were nights I didn't even make it back to the Camden guesthouse—that's why it seemed silly to pay rent and I bought the air mattress. I plan to move into your apartment when the barbecue is over tonight, Hutch, but there will still be nights when I'm sure I'll end up staying at the site, using the air mattress."

"You can't let him do this to you," Hutch said.

Maybe they did know about Seth and what had gone on with him. But how could they?

"If you let him, Dad will take your entire life and use it as his own," Ian added, letting her know that it wasn't Seth they were referring to.

"He's done it to both of us and now he's doing it to you with the training center," Hutch put in.

Her brothers went on to talk about how the bigger-than-life Morgan Kincaid might not be aware of just how much he demanded of his children, but that they'd both lost years and relationships and things that were important to them in the course of doing what their father wanted of them.

"There comes a time with him when you just have to stand up and say no," Hutch advised her. "Because if you don't, you don't get a life of your own."

"You know Hutch figured that out before I did," Ian contributed. "But I had to come to it myself with Jenna, with the land for the training facility. You've avoided his wrath before—"

"Because I'm the girl."

"Because you're the girl," Ian agreed. "But now that he's got you doing the center, we feel like we're watching you fall into the hole we had to fight our way out of."

"And we're hoping we can save you from it before it goes too far," Hutch put in.

"I'm fine," Lacey lied.

"No. You're doing a great job for him, but you're not fine," Hutch corrected. "Look in the mirror—you're pale as a ghost, there are circles under your eyes, I swear you look like you've lost ten pounds since the last time I saw you. And we had to double-team you and threaten you just to get you to come here today. You would have worked otherwise."

"The thing is," Ian said, "we just want you to learn from our mistakes. You have to draw the line with the old man because no matter how much you give, he'll want more."

"It's something we learned when he was drilling us for football when we were little kids. And no, it isn't easy to buck him, and he'll pull out all the stops to keep you doing what he wants."

"He'd say that I can't do the job. That he knew it all along."

"He would and he will," Ian confirmed. "But you can't let that get to you. I let what he said get to me for too long. I tried to please him at any cost for too long. You can work with Dad, for Dad, but it has to be you who draws the line and sticks to it, because he never will. He'll take all you've got and just want more, and you won't be left with anything for yourself."

Jenna and Issa came out the back door then, carrying trays full of appetizers, drinks and food to be grilled, effectively ending the intervention that Lacey was sure now didn't have anything to do with Seth.

But she couldn't help making a connection between what her brothers had said and what Seth had said to her that last Friday night at the office.

And it didn't help that she was sitting in Ian's backyard, with Ian who now had Jenna and Abby, with Hutch who now had Issa and Ash.

Her brothers had families. Lives. They had weathered storms with their father and absorbed his disapproval, his disparagement, his belittling. They had weathered years of separation from Morgan Kincaid.

Hutch and Ian had withstood the worst their father had dished out and pushed through it, gone beyond it, to find and have what they wanted. What made them happy.

And maybe she was really, really tired—no, there was no question about it, she *was* really, really tired—but she suddenly started to see something in the message of her brothers' intervention that they hadn't intended to give.

No one escaped Morgan Kincaid's criticism. No one was totally free of his narrow-mindedness or his biases. And no one could please him or win his approval unconditionally or for all time.

Her brothers might not have had to deal with their father's sexism, but they'd had their own burdens to bear with Morgan's expectations of them on the football field, in business, in personal lives he'd tried to use to his advantage.

And her burden to bear was that she *the girl.* She

was female. And Morgan Kincaid had archaic, macho opinions about what that meant. None of which were any more important than anything he'd said about Ian or Hutch along the way when they hadn't done what suited him.

But she was killing herself to change her father's mind. To prove he was wrong.

And worse than that, she was turning her back on what she'd found with Seth to do it.

Seth wasn't her father or Dominic. He hadn't asked her to stop doing what she was doing, he hadn't ignored what was important to her or expected her to fit some idea he had of what a woman should do or be. All he'd done was ask her to do what Ian and Hutch had just advised her to do: put work into perspective, not let it take up every minute of every day—and night. Not let it be all there was to her life.

Seth had asked her to explore what she *wanted*. What made her happiest.

And she'd been afraid of doing that because if what she wanted was him and a life with him and a family with him, then her father would ride in on his high horse and say that he'd been right all along.

But so what? So what if he rode that high horse into a life she had with Seth? Into a life that was always like Founder's Day weekend had been? Into a life as happy as what Hutch had found with Issa, as happy as what Ian had found with Jenna? Wasn't that happiness—feeling the way she felt when she was with Seth—the real victory? Not that she could prove her father wrong or make her point, but that she had Seth and all he was offering?

How could I have been so dumb? she asked herself. Seth was amazing. He was gorgeous, he was smart, he was funny and sexy and strong. He was his own man, a man who had shunned expectations that had been placed on him as a Camden because he'd had the wisdom to know himself and what he needed in life in order to find his own way.

And she was empty without him.

She'd filled every single hour since ending things with him with work or fitful sleep. She'd frantically done anything she could to keep from even thinking about him. But the truth was that in spite of any of that there was a huge hole in her heart that she couldn't fill, that never went away.

She wanted Seth. She wanted to be with him. No job, no point to prove, no worry of an I-told-you-so, carried more weight than that. Nothing and no one carried more weight than that. She wanted him. She wanted a life with him. A future with him. Kids with him.

If she hadn't already lost any hope of that...

"I have to go!" she announced before she even knew she was going to say anything.

"Are you okay?"

"Are you sick?"

Lacey's laugh at her brothers' questions was slightly batty. She knew she really, really was tired.

But what she said was "You guys are right—in more ways than you know. And I need to take care of something—if it isn't already too late. So I'm not going to stay for dinner."

Ian and Hutch both looked worried and along with Issa and Jenna, they all tried to persuade Lacey to stay.

But they couldn't.

Because she had something so, so much more important to do than to eat a hamburger and an ear of corn.

Chapter Twelve

Lacey was anxious and eager and scared and worried and in a rush to get to Seth as soon as she could. She didn't want to lose another moment and risk that he might meet someone else or decide he was better off without her.

But she also didn't want him to see her looking like she'd showered and shampooed her hair for the last ten days under a barely warm drizzle of water and slept on an air mattress for far fewer hours than she'd needed.

He was likely at one Labor Day function or another and not home anyway, she decided, so she could take a little time to spruce up.

When she reached Hutch's duplex, she used the key he'd given her to let herself in and go straight up the stairs to the upper-floor apartment with her suitcase in hand. She dropped the suitcase in the middle of the living-room floor as soon as she went into the apartment, opened it up and took out the only thing she had to wear that didn't look like it belonged at a construction site—a short yellow A-line crepe sundress that was plain, sleeveless and shapeless.

She knew it wouldn't be sex appeal that won the day with that, but it was her only choice.

She found a hanger in the closet in the bedroom, hung the dress on it and took it with her into the bathroom, hoping the steam from her shower would rid it of wrinkles.

Then she took her first good shower in days and washed her hair so thoroughly her scalp started to hurt before she rinsed it.

There was nothing to be done with her hair but to let it air-dry because she hadn't packed her hair dryer. But she counted herself lucky to have enough natural wave and body to still wear the blond mass down once it dried on its own.

Even though she hated the time it was taking, she was careful with her makeup, using concealer on the dark circles under her eyes, blush to add some color to her face, and just enough mascara to draw attention to her lashes and away from the evidence of her lack of sleep.

She didn't have the bra she needed to wear with the dress, and since the ones she had would have left the straps showing, she went without, wearing only lace bikini panties under the well-lined shift.

Then she did a couple of fierce shakes of the dress to rid it of any lingering wrinkles, judged it presentable, and put it on.

Once she'd slipped her sandals on, she was ready to go.

Taking with her so many butterflies in her stomach

that she had to pause to breathe deeply in an effort to calm them before they made her sick.

Just go find him... Maybe it will be okay...

Or maybe it wouldn't. Maybe it was already too late...

No, she couldn't think that, she told herself.

She couldn't.

But still the thought lingered as she grabbed her keys, hurried out of the apartment and headed for the Camden ranch.

She'd had her assistant notify Seth of two things during the last week—one that she would have all of her belongings out of his guesthouse by Labor Day, and two, that she would appreciate it if he would give her specifics on what he was willing to do on the issue of the road she needed to put through his property.

She'd received Seth's response via a messenger of his own—the Camdens would sell her the strip of land that she required at a price that was reasonable enough to please even her father, and with no conditions, exceptions, exclusions or contingencies despite the fact that it would be bisecting a parcel of their property.

There had been no comment about Lacey vacating the guesthouse.

As she drove to the ranch, she worried that that had been because it suited Seth just fine for her to get out. And that it might be an indication that he wouldn't be so welcoming of her when she showed up.

It didn't occur to her until she turned onto the road that led to Seth's house that he might be having a Labor Day barbecue of his own. An entire party that she might be crashing.

But since there were no cars to be seen when she

approached the house, she decided that wasn't going to be a problem.

So she pulled around to the garages and parked where she'd parked when she'd been staying there, opting to take the rear route into the houses again now.

Not only wasn't there a party going on in back, around the pool, but there also wasn't a single sign of Seth anywhere. In fact, the main house was locked up tight, and she went back to thinking that he was probably spending the holiday with friends. Hopefully male friends.

She considered using the time while she waited for him to return to pack what remained of her belongings in the guesthouse. Certainly a case could be made for it—if this didn't go well, it would be good to have all of her things cleared out, loaded in her car and ready to take with her.

But something about that just seemed so defeatist that she couldn't make herself do it. Instead she sat on the nearest lounger and decided to try to get her nerves under control while she waited for Seth.

Initially, she sat perched on the side of the lounger, her feet planted flat on the pool tiles, her spine straight, her hands in her lap.

But time passed and she could feel herself beginning to slump, so she swung her legs onto the lounger and sat back, her head still high and held away from the chair.

Then somehow her head fell back, too, and she started to look at the calm, clear blue water of the pool.

Then her eyes were burning so she closed them...

For only a minute, she told herself. She would close them for only a minute.

Or maybe for two...

"Lacey?"

Seth...

The man was insatiable.

But that was okay, because she wanted him, too. This really had been the very best way to close out Founder's Day weekend...

"Lacey? Wake up."

Founder's Day weekend? The power was out. They'd made love.

But they'd gone inside. Why did it feel like she was still outside?

It wasn't Founder's Day weekend.

It was Labor Day.

She wasn't supposed to be asleep!

Lacey jolted awake, realizing that somehow it had gotten dark. Very dark. And it seemed really late. And she felt like she'd been asleep for hours and hours.

And Seth was there—she could see him through sleep-blurred vision, wearing a gray polo shirt and jeans, sitting a few feet to the side of the lounger. On a suitcase?

"Oh… What time is it?" she muttered, struggling to get her bearings and recalling suddenly all that had gone on and why she was there.

"3:00 a.m."

"It's three o'clock in the morning?" She'd slept a long time. "And you're just coming home? With a suitcase?"

"I've been in Vegas with my brother and a couple of my cousins. They, uh… It's something we do for each other when it seems like there's a need…"

"A gambling need?"

"A need to get away to cheer one of us up…"

"Which one of you?" she asked artlessly, still fighting her way out of the heavy cloud of exhausted slumber.

"I think you know," he said somberly.

Lacey's vision finally came into focus and she took a closer look at Seth—disheveled hair, scruffy beard, circles under his blue eyes, too.

"What are you doing here?" he asked. Then, before she could answer, he said, "Oh, yeah, it was Labor Day, wasn't it? You said you'd get the rest of your stuff from the guesthouse. What did you do, sit down to catch your breath between loads and fall asleep?"

"No!" she said, sounding slightly panicked that he thought that, that he was so accepting of that explanation for why she was there. "That's not what I came for at all."

She'd raised her head from the back of the lounger when she'd come awake but now she sat up completely, realizing that her short skirt was high on her thigh.

She tugged at the hem to pull it down as she swung her feet to the tile, wondering where her sandals had gone even as she caught Seth's gaze dropping to her legs for a moment before he yanked it away.

"What did you come for?" he asked then, a deep frown pulling his brows toward each other.

"My brothers twisted my arm to get me to a barbecue at Ian's house today… Yesterday, I guess… And, well, it was eye-opening."

Seth didn't say anything to that. He merely went on watching her, giving no encouragement or even an indication that he was glad she was there. Instead the expression on his heartbreakingly handsome face was still dark, leery, distant.

But Lacey knew this was all her fault, that it was

up to her to fix it, so she went on to tell him just how her eyes had been opened earlier and the realizations she'd come to.

"I don't want to turn around one day, alone, with nothing but some point I've proven. Seeing my brothers happy, with their new families—Dad not being a factor in any of that—made me know that I just want to have a life, my own life, too. That I should be able to."

"Where do the jobs fit in?" Seth asked with some skepticism coloring his tone.

"To tell you the truth, I'm not sure. I've been thinking about you, about us, about having a future together—"

"*Before* thinking about work?"

He was skeptical, all right.

"*Instead* of thinking about work," Lacey said. "I know I want to go on with the clothing line because I enjoy that—it's mine, it's all mine, and I want to keep doing that. But it's manageable. And when it comes to the training center? I already feel like I've been working on that for ten years. And I don't enjoy anything about it. I know my father will say that I couldn't handle it—"

"But you can because you have."

"That won't matter to him. He'll still say that construction isn't a woman's work. But I somehow reached a place where I don't care. It *isn't* a job for me because I don't want to do it. Maybe he'll give the project back to Ian—if Ian wants it. Or maybe he'll have to do it himself—he'll get to have his say over every nail and splinter and clod of dirt that has to be moved."

"So he might as well be there doing it himself."

"All I know is that it's you I want, Seth," Lacey said, her voice going quiet all of a sudden and catching in her throat as she watched him stand up. She worried that he might be fidgety because he was about to tell her it didn't matter anymore what she wanted.

And in response to that thought, she stood, too, as if that would make her position stronger.

"For the first time," she continued, "there's something that's only about the one person I care more about than anyone I've ever cared about before—you. There's something that's only about being with you. About what we have when we're together. I know that essentially what Dominic wanted—my full attention—"

"Except that he wanted you to give up everything else and I didn't ask that of you."

"I know. And that's a very big deal to me. But when I thought about basically having the kind of life with Dominic that I've been thinking about having with you, I didn't want it. He wasn't that important to me. I didn't have the same kind of feelings for him. But when I think about having that life with you... It's exactly what I want. It's *all* that I want. *You're* what I want. And *everything* else takes second place."

His hands were on his hips. He switched most of his weight onto one of them and stared at her. But again he didn't say anything, and Lacey's heart was beating fast and hard with the worry that he just couldn't accept what she was saying.

She stepped nearer to him, facing him, and looked up into his eyes. "And you don't have to become the biggest football fan ever," she told him. "It means a lot to me that you'd be willing to go to such lengths in order to fit into my family, but you don't have to. Because you and I are enough. For the first time, with you, I can see myself building something of my own. A family of my own. A life of my own. All my own. And it's more than enough—it's the way it should be."

Seth went on staring into her eyes for another long moment before he said, "I love you, Lacey."

"I love you, too," she said, still unsure if that was the segue to something.

"I don't want you to give up anything you don't want to give up. I just want you. And time with you."

"You can have all you want," she assured.

"I want you to marry me," he said as if it were a test.

"I want you to marry me," she countered, as relief began to seep in and she started to feel a little cocky.

"I want to have kids with you."

"I want to have kids with *you,*" she said.

"I want to grow old with you."

"Go ahead, but I decided a long time ago that once I hit thirty-five I was sticking with it from then on," she joked.

He finally cracked a smile, and it was the best thing Lacey had ever seen.

"I'll be eighty and you'll be my still-thirty-five-year-old bride?" he asked.

"And I'm going to have to count on you to look like December so I can pull off looking like May."

He laughed. A sound good enough to go with the smile. So good that for no reason Lacey could fathom, it brought tears to her eyes.

"I'll ask for extra wrinkles with every birthday from here on," he promised.

Then his arms came around her and he pulled her to him, so tightly that she had to turn her head. Her cheek was pressed to his chest as she hugged him back.

"I was afraid I wasn't going to get this," he said then

in a grave voice. "And no amount of Vegas or my brother or my cousins could cheer me up."

"I'm sorry," Lacey whispered. "I'm sorry I was so stubborn and stupid and blind and slow."

He loosened his grip on her and veered back, looking down at her while she peered up at him. "Watch it, I don't let anybody say those kinds of things about my fiancée."

Lacey laughed a little at that, finally conquering that threat of tears as she looked up at him and saw what ravages her actions had wreaked.

"You look tired," she said.

This time his smile was devilish. "I had a nap on the plane, so I'm not too tired," he said before he kissed her a kiss that, at first, only said hello.

But then it went on to say so much more, to renew and rekindle, refresh and reawaken things in Lacey that she'd had to suppress for the last ten days in order to survive.

A kiss that reminded her of what she had with this man, of how much he stirred in her, of the fact that she only felt truly complete when she was with him.

Then he ended that kiss, stepped back and dipped a little. The next thing Lacey knew she was flung over one of those broad shoulders and watching his divine derriere from a very odd perspective while cool night air touched hers.

"Oh, this dress is short!" she screeched.

"I'll say," Seth agreed, patting her exposed rump as he sauntered around the pool to the main house, unlocked one set of the French doors and let them in.

He didn't so much as pause to turn on a light, taking her to his bedroom where he unceremoniously deposited her onto his big bed and then joined her there.

Cowboy boots were the first to come off, but after that clothes flew, mouths came together and hands reacquainted themselves with tender flesh.

Desire and arousal ran rampant through Lacey with Seth's every wondrous touch. Needs grew and made demands, and a hunger that had been simmering in her for ten days went to a full boil as she ran her own palms over that exquisitely masculine body that she could never have lived without.

They made wild, passionate love. Wild, passionate love that spoke of how much they'd missed it and each other, of all the glories yet to come for them in a lifetime of lovemaking.

Once their peaks had been reached, leaving them both sated and satiated and their reunion finally and firmly sealed, Seth collapsed with his back to the mattress and pulled Lacey to his side, offering his chest as her pillow, his arms as her blanket.

"I love you, Lacey," he said, pressing another kiss into her hair.

"I love you, Seth," she answered, kissing his chest.

"Will you come with me next weekend to Denver for my grandmother's birthday? Can we announce our wedding then?"

"I'm at your disposal," she said. "But is your family going to hate me for causing your need to be cheered up this weekend?"

"My family will see that you've made me the happiest guy on the planet and love you for it. The bigger problem might be getting us out of this bed in time to go…"

"You want to spend the next four days in bed?"

"What a great idea!"

Lacey laughed, but in truth, the thought of spending four days in bed with him suited her just fine.

She said, "Get some sleep and we'll talk about it. I might be persuaded to take tomorrow off...."

"Hmm... I'll have to think of a way...." he muttered. She could tell he was already drifting off.

That was all right, though, because she was perfectly content to lie in his arms and just bask in what she'd found with him.

A sense of home.

Of things being right.

Of being exactly where she belonged.

And of finally, once and for all, discovering what she wanted for herself that didn't have anything to do with her father or the Kincaid Corporation.

Finally, once and for all, discovering what she wanted for herself.

And getting it.

* * * * *

COMING NEXT MONTH from Harlequin
Special Edition®
AVAILABLE JUNE 19, 2012

#2197 THE LAST SINGLE MAVERICK
Montana Mavericks: Back in the Saddle
Christine Rimmer

Steadfastly single cowboy Jason Traub asks Jocelyn Bennings to
accompany him to his family reunion to avoid any blind dates his family
has planned for him. Little does he know that she's a runaway bride—and
that he's about to lose his heart to her!

#2198 THE PRINCESS AND THE OUTLAW
Royal Babies
Leanne Banks

Princess Pippa Devereaux has never defied her family except when it
comes to Nic Lafitte. But their feuding families won't be enough to keep
these star-crossed lovers apart.

#2199 HIS TEXAS BABY
Men of the West
Stella Bagwell

The relationship of rival horse breeders Kitty Cartwright and
Liam Donovan takes a whole new turn when an unplanned pregnancy
leads to an unplanned romance.

#2200 A MARRIAGE WORTH FIGHTING FOR
McKinley Medics
Lilian Darcy

The last thing Alicia McKinley expects when she leaves her husband, MJ,
is for him to put up a fight for their marriage. What surprises her even
more is that she starts falling back in love with him.

#2201 THE CEO'S UNEXPECTED PROPOSAL
Reunion Brides
Karen Rose Smith

High school crushes Dawson Barrett and Mikala Conti are reunited when
Dawson asks her to help his traumatized son recover from an accident.
When sparks fly and a baby on the way complicates things even more,
can this couple make it work?

#2202 LITTLE MATCHMAKERS
Jennifer Greene

Being a single parent is hard, but Garnet Cottrell and Tucker MacKinnon
have come up with a "kid-swapping" plan to help give their boys a more
well-rounded upbringing. But unbeknownst to their parents the boys
have a matchmaking plan of their own.

You can find more information on upcoming Harlequin® titles,
free excerpts and more at www.HarlequinInsideRomance.com.

HSECNM0612

REQUEST YOUR FREE BOOKS!

2 FREE NOVELS PLUS 2 FREE GIFTS!

SPECIAL EDITION

Life, Love & Family

YES! Please send me 2 FREE Harlequin® Special Edition novels and my 2 FREE gifts (gifts are worth about $10). After receiving them, if I don't wish to receive any more books, I can return the shipping statement marked "cancel." If I don't cancel, I will receive 6 brand-new novels every month and be billed just $4.49 per book in the U.S. or $5.24 per book in Canada. That's a saving of at least 14% off the cover price! It's quite a bargain! Shipping and handling is just 50¢ per book in the U.S. and 75¢ per book in Canada.* I understand that accepting the 2 free books and gifts places me under no obligation to buy anything. I can always return a shipment and cancel at any time. Even if I never buy another book, the two free books and gifts are mine to keep forever.

235/335 HDN FEGF

Name	(PLEASE PRINT)	
Address		Apt. #
City	State/Prov.	Zip/Postal Code

Signature (if under 18, a parent or guardian must sign)

Mail to the **Reader Service:**
IN U.S.A.: P.O. Box 1867, Buffalo, NY 14240-1867
IN CANADA: P.O. Box 609, Fort Erie, Ontario L2A 5X3

Not valid for current subscribers to Harlequin Special Edition books.

Want to try two free books from another line?
Call 1-800-873-8635 or visit www.ReaderService.com.

* Terms and prices subject to change without notice. Prices do not include applicable taxes. Sales tax applicable in N.Y. Canadian residents will be charged applicable taxes. Offer not valid in Quebec. This offer is limited to one order per household. All orders subject to credit approval. Credit or debit balances in a customer's account(s) may be offset by any other outstanding balance owed by or to the customer. Please allow 4 to 6 weeks for delivery. Offer available while quantities last.

Your Privacy—The Reader Service is committed to protecting your privacy. Our Privacy Policy is available online at www.ReaderService.com or upon request from the Reader Service.

We make a portion of our mailing list available to reputable third parties that offer products we believe may interest you. If you prefer that we not exchange your name with third parties, or if you wish to clarify or modify your communication preferences, please visit us at www.ReaderService.com/consumerschoice or write to us at Reader Service Preference Service, P.O. Box 9062, Buffalo, NY 14269. Include your complete name and address.

HSE11B

Harlequin®

SPECIAL EDITION

Life, Love and Family

USA TODAY bestselling author

Leanne Banks

begins a heartwarming new miniseries

Royal Babies

When princess Pippa Devereaux learns that the mother of Texas tycoon and longtime business rival Nic Lafitte is terminally ill she secretly goes against her family's wishes and helps Nic fulfill his mother's dying wish. Nic is awed by Pippa's kindness and quickly finds himself falling for her. But can their love break their long-standing family feud?

THE PRINCESS
AND THE OUTLAW

Available July 2012!
Wherever books are sold.

HSE65680

*Harlequin® American Romance® presents a
brand-new miniseries* HARTS OF THE RODEO.

*Enjoy a sneak peek at AIDAN: LOYAL COWBOY
from favorite author Cathy McDavid.*

Ace walked unscathed to the gate and sighed quietly. On
the other side he paused to look at Midnight.

The horse bobbed his head.

Yeah, I agree. Ace grinned to himself, feeling as if he,
too, had passed a test. *You're coming home to Thunder
Ranch with me.*

Scanning the nearby vicinity, he searched out his mother.
She wasn't standing where he'd left her. He spotted her
several feet away, conversing with his uncle Joshua and
cousin Duke who'd accompanied Ace and his mother to the
sale.

He'd barely started toward them when Flynn McKinley
crossed his path.

A jolt of alarm brought him to a grinding halt. She'd
come to the auction after all!

What now?

"Hi." He tried to move and couldn't. The soft ground
pulled at him, sucking his boots down into the muck. He
was trapped.

Served him right.

She stared at him in silence, tendrils of corn-silk-yellow
hair peeking out from under her cowboy hat.

Memories surfaced. Ace had sifted his hands through
that hair and watched, mesmerized, as the soft strands
coiled around his fingers like spun gold.

Then, not two hours later, he'd abruptly left her bedside,
hurting her with his transparent excuses.

She stared at him now with the same pained expression she'd worn that morning.

"Flynn, I'm sorry," he offered lamely.

"For what exactly?" She crossed her arms in front of her, glaring at him through slitted blue eyes. "Slinking out of my room before my father discovered you'd spent the night or acting like it never happened?"

What exactly is Ace sorry for? Find out in
AIDAN: LOYAL COWBOY.

Available this July wherever books are sold.

This summer, celebrate everything Western
with Harlequin® Books!

www.Harlequin.com/Western

Debut author

Kathy Altman

takes you on a moving journey
of forgiveness and second chances.

One year after losing her husband in Afghanistan,
Parker Dean finds Corporal Reid Macfarland at her
door with a heartfelt confession and a promise to save
her family business. Although Reid is the last person
Parker should trust her livelihood to, she finds herself
captivated by his silent courage. Together,
can they learn to forgive and love again?

The Other Soldier

Available July 2012 wherever books are sold.

This summer, celebrate everything Western
with Harlequin® Books!

www.Harlequin.com/Western